# THE TREE LORD
# OF IMETEN

by

TOM PURDOM

D1232412

ACE BOOKS, INC.
1120 Avenue of the Americas
New York, N.Y. 10036

# I

Joe Persa's body lay in the dirt less than twenty meters from the tractor. He saw it every time he peered around the front tread. Blood stained all the ground around it and there was a big hump underneath the jacket. The metal-tipped arrow, released at close range, had smashed through clothing, muscle, bone and heart as if it were an Eighteenth Century cannon ball crashing into wood, and when Joe had stopped in midstride and toppled forward, the weight of his body had pushed the point out his back.

His lips curled back every time he looked at it. Anger was the only response death ever provoked from him. Five years ago, when this planet had finally killed his mother and his young sister, his anger had sent him stalking across the plateau late at night with a fury which his sixteen year old mind had naively assumed was the unexceedable limit of the indignation a human being can endure. And this morning, when he had looked out the window and seen his father and his best friend crumple before the rifles of Emile Detterman and Ben Keler, his outraged bellow had frozen everyone standing in the street. The arrows had flown from his bow as if he were a vengeful god hurling thunderbolts. He hated death—even when he had dealt it himself, even when he wanted to kill the men who had dealt it to his friends.

He peered underneath the curve of the front tread. Raising his eyes from the body, he inspected the open ground between the tractor and the buildings a hundred meters away. To his nearsighted eyes the buildings looked fuzzy. The plastic windows looked like black holes, and if he had never seen them before, he wouldn't have known the eight two-story buildings on his left were gray metal, and the thirty one-story buildings on his right were gray stone. To him, the huge bulk of the spherical orbit-to-ground vehicle two kilometers away was a shapeless black cloud. The forest beyond the vehicle was a dark smear which could have been anything.

The only detectable sounds were the wind and the faint roar of the waterfall at the end of the plateau. He assumed no one was working in the farm on the other side of the buildings, since he couuldn't hear voices and both the tractors were in this shed with him, but if they had been working he couldn't have seen them.

Most of the people in the settlement were hiding. After Emile's gang killed him, they would creep into the open, accept the new leadership, and continue their lives until the next struggle for power broke out. What else could they do? If everyone could be that apathetic about who played the roll of leader, his father and Walt Sumi would still be alive.

It had now been several minutes since a rifle bullet had last cracked above the tractor. It had been almost an hour since they had last tried to rush him.

The shed he was hiding in was isolated from the rest of the settlement. A sheer cliff protected his back, and they could attack him from the front only by sniping at him or by rushing him across open, leveled ground. The arrow in Joe Persa's heart had apparently taught them even a hail of rifle bullets couldn't keep him from killing whoever volunteered to make the assault.

He slid behind the tractor and crouched along it toward the other end. The shadows of the buildings had indicated it was now early afternoon, five hours since the sun had first risen above the western horizon. He assumed they would now wait four more hours and rush him in the dark, but he couldn't be sure. He had to watch both ends of the tractor if he wanted to cover all the ground in front of him. He didn't want to be taken by surprise. When he died, he would fall hurling death.

He was a deadly archer in spite of his eyes. He had killed or seriously injured at least two others besides Joe. His father had insisted he get along without glasses and learn how to compensate. They couldn't be dependent, his father had felt, on the technology of a human civilization which was now eighteen light years away and which none of them, hopefully, would ever contact again. This isolated plateau on Delta Pavonis II was going to be their entire world for many decades; if they wanted to survive they should use, as much as possible, only what could be grown or built here, or the equipment from the starship which wouldn't wear out before they could expect to build replacements.

He straightened up cautiously and glanced over the top of the tractor. Something moved beside the nearest building.

He ducked and threw himself flat. His right arm reached behind his shoulder for an arrow. He wiggled forward and peered under the curve of the rear tread.

Someone was walking toward the shed. He would wait until they got as close as Joe had been.

He blinked the sweat out of his eyes. Under his loose white shirt and loose white pants his body felt oily and dirty. Normally at this time of day he would have stripped to his shorts and given himself a sponge bath.

He pulled his head in when the fuzzy human figure was half the distance between the buildings and Joe's body. While he was watching it, the others could be approaching him across the ground he couldn't see from this end of the tractor. He crawled back to the other end and looked out.

Sunlight flashed on red hair. His eyes finally detected the slight lurch to the left every time the approaching figure made a step.

His heart jumped. *Joanne!* The face was still a blur, but no one else in the settlement had red hair and walked like that.

His eyes searched the buildings for a flash of sunlight on gun metal. They might be using her for a decoy. She could even have decided she should help them kill him. In this universe anything was possible.

She stopped well beyond Joe's body. He could imagine the expression on her face. She and Joe had been friends since they were children on the starship.

She cupped her hands over her mouth. "Harold! I want to talk to you. Please let me talk to you."

He pulled his head in. "Don't come any closer!"

"I've been talking to Emile. He's willing to let you leave

the settlement. He says he'll give you food and equipment."

He crawled to the other end of the tractor and looked out. The urge to kill her flashed through his mind. He wasn't interested in living. Anger was the only emotion left in his body.

"Go away!"

"Emile doesn't want to kill you. Please listen to me. He knows more people will die if they try to attack you."

He crawled back to the front end of the tractor. Holding out her hands, she stepped forward.

She stopped. "Don't you trust me?"

"Go back!"

She limped toward him. "I won't let you die. Listen to reason."

His hand tightened on his bow. He squinted at the buildings. They could have a dozen rifles trained on him. He lived his life in a fog.

She stepped past the body. The bulk of the tractor hid her from his eyes.

He rose to a crouch and jumped backward into the shadows. The bowstring slid smoothly into the notch of an arrow.

She limped around the tractor. Her eyes widened. "*Harold!*"

They stared at each other. The bow was at the level of his chest. The arrow was half drawn.

Her eyes searched his face. She shook her head slowly. "What have they done to you?"

He shifted the arrow so it pointed at the ground. The bulging, overdeveloped muscles of his arms and shoulders were rigid with tension.

Why couldn't he go back in time? Why couldn't he reach through thirteen hours and grab his friends's shoulder and tell him not to go out in the morning?

Her voice trembled. "Emile says they'll line up out of bow range without their weapons. They can't let you stay here, but they don't want to fight."

He glanced out the front of the shed. He couldn't believe she would hurt him, but she was a very trusting girl. While she was distracting him, they could be closing in from both sides.

"Where will I go? Back to Earth?"

"I know it's sickening. They're the ones that ought to leave." She wiped the sweat off her face. Tears filled her eyes. "It's better than dying, isn't it? Don't you want to live?"

He gestured with the bow. "Go stand in front of the tractor. I'll talk to you there."

"Don't you trust me?"

"While I'm standing back here, they could be doing anything."

She buried her face in her hands. Her shoulders trembled as she stumbled outside.

He ran forward and crouched behind the tractor. He bobbed up and glanced over the top and then he stretched out and peered under the front tread again.

"Harold?"

"I'm here."

"We've got a whole world. There must be someplace we can go."

"We?"

"You don't think I can stay here, do you?"

"Do you think you can live down there?"

"Don't make me stay here! If you won't do it for yourself, do it for me!"

He pictured the two of them trying to survive in the forest at the foot of the plateau—separated from their own society; exposed to unknown animals and dangers; dead from starvation if they lost their food supply; one half blind,

the other crippled by the way her muscles had adapted
to a gravitational field twenty percent stronger than the
gravitational field in which the human body had evolved;
nagged at every step by the potential danger of the unknown creatures who built the great towers and statues
which rose above the forest—

His lips curled. Why didn't they attack? Give him one
more shot.

"Don't make me live with three graves," Joanne said. "Be
yourself." Her voice quivered. "Do you think they would
have wanted a pile of bodies for a monument?"

She started crying. He stared at Joe's body and then
looked beyond it to where the plateau ended in a thou-
sand-meter drop. The forest loomed in his consciousness.

Walt stood in front of him, shaking his head. *What are
you trying to do?*

He couldn't think. It had all happened too fast. He had
been all set to die—he had been dead already—and now
she was asking him to stand up and do something.

"How long do you think you can stay alive in the forest?"
She stifled her crying. "I'd rather die there than commit
suicide here." She hesitated. "I can't stay here. When I
went in to talk to them—to them I'm with you now. If I
stay here, they'll probably kill me, too."

"Did you think about that before you talked to them?"

"I couldn't let you die!"

He scowled. *Why not?*

He couldn't say it. She made his uncontrolled savagery
seem shameful. She had risked her own life to get him out
of this. It had probably never even occurred to her he
might not want to live.

"I know how you feel," she said. "I think I feel the same
way. Walt meant as much to me as he meant to you. I'd
like to crawl off someplace and never see another human

face. But we've got to go on living. What you're doing isn't right. You don't believe in it yourself."

He crawled to the other end of the tractor. He checked the ground briefly and then he crawled back.

"What's Emile going to do?" he asked. "Is he going to stay on the plateau?"

She caught her breath. "I don't know. They haven't said anything."

"Is he in charge or Ben?"

"He seems to be in charge."

"That won't last long. What did they say they'd give us?"

"They said they'd give us whatever we need."

"Rifles?"

She hesitated. "I didn't ask them."

"Cheese fungus? Seeds? Rabbits? Knives?"

"Emil said they'd give us anything we need to survive."

"A cart?"

"Can we use one in the forest?"

"If we can't, we'll abandon it." he thought. Through his anger and grief old emotions were beginning to assert themselves. When his mother and sister had died, his rage eventually had been transformed into an attitude which had served many men before him. You couldn't defeat death by shaking your fist at it, or by pretending it wasn't real or that it didn't matter—or by lying down and letting it kill you. You defeated death by living as long as you could, and by doing things death couldn't destroy. "We'll need an anti-grav platform to get down the cliff. Tell Emile they can send a girl with us to get the platform back up. If he won't give it to us—tell him I'll stay here. I mean that. Don't let him think I don't. If you don't get the platform, the deal's off."

"You won't try climbing down the east face of the cliff?"

"And have them shoot us from a platform? They'll still probably come after us. I'd rather go up in the mountains, but in the forest we'll have some cover over us."

"They really want us to go, Harold. You haven't seen them. They've had as much as they can stomach."

"We have to assume the worst. This is no time to be trusting." He wiped the sweat off his brow. "Let me think. Clothes . . . water purifiers . . . Ask for some nails."

He was beginning to feel hungry and tired. It would be morning before they could rest and he knew he had probably eaten his last hot meal for many days.

Why hadn't she left him alone? They'd be lucky if they survived a month. If he ever returned to this plateau, at least two people would pay with their lives for everything he was about to endure.

For a moment his churning brain threw up a scene he had never witnessed, but which had been described to him at least once a year since he had been old enough to understand: his father, thirty-nine years ago, looked back at Earth as the starship made its hurried escape. That had been the most bitter moment of his father's life. For the usual reasons—power, fear, greed—the masters of psychological manipulation had turned the Earth into a world where no human being could be sure his thoughts were his own. The colony on the moon where the starship had been constructed had been the last outpost of freedom, and everyone there had known the psych engineers would eventually tamper with their minds, too, if they didn't escape before the government decided their freedom was no longer useful. Gathering all their courage, outfitting the ship in twenty-four hours of frantic labor, they had left in a blaze of gunfire as the police closed in, and plunged into the black gulfs between the stars, promising themselves they would find a world where men could be free.

Soon he would be looking back at the settlement as his father had looked back at Earth.

## II

AT NIGHT a thin mist covered the bottom of the forest. The planet was much wetter and hotter than Earth. Ocean covered almost eighty percent of its surface, and it was twenty-three million miles closer to a sun which was only a few hundred degrees cooler than the sun which warmed Earth. During the hot, nine-hour day, immense quantities of water evaporated from the sprawling ocean and were trapped between the mountains and the southern coast.

Joanne pulled one handle of the cart and he pulled the other. No underbrush grew in this part of the forest—the trees blocked out most of the sunlight—but the ground fought their muscles every turn of the cart's wheels. In the darkness and the fog they stumbled over roots, loose rocks, and pitted, uneven ground. Fear of the night and the unknown stiffened their legs and shortened their steps.

Cut off from all social organization, Harold felt naked and defenseless. The animal noises coming from the trees unnerved him. His free hand clutched the nail-studded club he had made as if he expected to be attacked at any minute.

They had plunged due south when they left the antigravity platform and then they had turned east. He wanted

14

to stay close to the mountains so they could eventually leave the forest and camp in higher, more open territory. What they would do after that he didn't know. He couldn't think that far ahead. He would find a hiding place for them and then he would rest and brood and sooner or later he would begin thinking about going on with his life.

What did a man do when he was no longer part of a community? He had been studying to be a biologist, the scientific vocation the settlement needed most, and the indispensable element in his vision of a happy, meaningful life was a picture of himself doing something others would find useful or interesting. He couldn't imagine life without some kind of work.

They had killed his friend and his father, and then, as if they were doing him a favor, they had robbed him of the thing he needed most—the chance to accomplish something he could consider meaningful. In one day they had come as close to killing him as they could without actually sending a bullet smashing through his brain.

Something shrieked behind him. He let go of the cart handle. Passing the club to his right hand, he whirled. "That was on the ground."

In the cart the rabbits stirred restlessly. Something knocked rhythmically and he realized it was Joanne's club banging against the side of the cart.

He blinked at the darkness. In nine years no human had ever left the plateau. Anything could prowl this forest. After the refugees crowded into the starship had decided the towers and statues looming over the trees had to be structures built by intelligent beings, his father had argued monotonously that caution was the only responsible policy when you were dealing with the unknown. There had been some violent arguments but in the end his father's faction had

15

won out. As the last free human minds left in the universe, they couldn't afford to take any risks.

He could still remember every detail of the bitter moment when they had orbited the planet and learned that, after spending thirty years in space and visiting two star systems, the first habitable planet they had discovered was —against all the odds—apparently already inhabited. They had thought about going on to another star, but thirty years in a spaceship, with two hundred and sixty people living in a space originally planned for a hundred, had been as much as most of them could tolerate.

He listened. Even if he heard something, he couldn't be sure he would interpet it correctly. On Earth a predator would have moved in silently, or they might have heard the faint padding of cushioned paws, or claws scratching on stone or bark, but here a predator might have evolved in ways no human could hope to imagine. The birds and small animals he had studied on the plateau had differed from Earth life just enough that anything had to be considered possible.

He turned around and gripped the handle. "Let's go. Are you getting tired?"

"I'm all right. I'll be ready to eat pretty soon."

"I'm getting hungry, too." Since morning he had eaten nothing but the soup and the pound of uncooked steak-plant she had brought him after she went to tell Emile he accepted the bargain. Even a hunk of cheese fungus seemed appetizing. "Don't talk much. We might as well keep going, but I want to listen."

"It sounded a little human, didn't it?"

"That's what I thought."

He checked their course against his wrist compass. His stomach felt nervous. If only he had a rifle! They had even refused to give him seeds for growing explosives.

16

The cartwheels creaked at his back. In the distance he could still hear the faint roar of the waterfall. Two hours more and they could stop to sleep. He'd take the first guard. She must be ready to collapse.

He glanced at her. Their eyes met and she made herself smile.

For the second time that day he thought, remotely, of the two of them alone in their shelter. He was too tense, dirty and tired to feel anything more than a faint memory of desire.

For several months now something had been growing between them. She was a companionable girl, a natural third when he and Walt got their weekly chance to sit around drinking home-made beer. Something in his personality responded to her basic serenity. He had been thinking about asking her to live with him. To keep the settlement growing, and the gene pool varied, every woman was supposed to have children by several men, but most of the women seemed to end up living with one man for years at a time.

At twenty-two she had been the oldest childless girl in the settlement. She lost two babies in a row and both the obstetricians had agreed she should let her system rest for a year.

Ahead of them something yapped several times. He froze. Again he let go of the handle and passed the club to his right hand. The cart swayed slightly, unbalanced on top of a bump, and Joanne pulled it forward and steadied it.

He couldn't be sure, but to him the yapping had sounded as if it were coming from the same kind of voice as the shriek.

"If it's the same thing," Joanne murmured, "it moved awfully fast."

"Maybe we'd better stop."

"Couldn't it be a carrion eater? Didn't jackals make that kind of noise?"

"We'll keep away from the trees. Make it cross open ground. It won't do much, but . . ."

He shrugged. His voice trailed off. He picked up his handle and they started forward.

In the daytime the vistas in the forest would have been at least a hundred yards. He wondered if he should have his bow ready instead of his club. If something resembling a lion or a panther attacked them during the day, even with his eyes he could probably shoot it before it reached them. Even at night, an obscure shape moving in the mist, or the noise of a charge, might give him time to string an arrow before the predator leaped.

He decided to keep the club. The bow would be better against some things, but the club would be useful against anything.

They edged the cart to the right so they could pass between two looming tree trunks with plenty of open space on all sides. His eyes scanned the lowest branches, long, massive beams nearly twenty meters from the forest floor. The trees in this forest had branches as high above the ground as forty meters, which could have supported his weight. As the noise overhead indicated, most of the life went on in the dense canopy of intertwining leaves and branches.

His biologist's mind wondered what the predators in this forest lived on. On Earth the big carnivores had lived primarily in the grasslands, feeding on the big, fast herbivores who browsed on the grass. Here, where there were no grasslands on the entire planet, any carnivores who lived on the ground would have to feed on creatures who browsed on the leaves, as giraffes had on Earth, or on creatures who rooted for nuts and insects. If they were being stalked by a carnivore, then they should also be alert for things that could trample them.

Why hadn't they seen any? They had walked at least ten kilometers. Were they being followed by humans?

He studied each branch as they trudged under it. Predators could live in the trees, too. And there was one unpredictable factor which couldn't be ignored and which could invalidate any reasoning based on the laws of nature: intelligence. The nearest statues and towers were at least two hundred kilometers from here, but for all he knew they could be walking in a carefully controlled park.

They walked for another hour and then they stopped to rest. They sat back to back on top of the cart, with their clubs by their right hands and his bow and two arrows in easy reach. They had heard the yapping twice more, but they had still seen no animal life bigger than small creatures and birds and a huge moth which had flapped out of a tree and drifted across their path.

He nibbled on a chunk of cheese fungus. "We'll camp in another hour. I'll take the first guard period."

"You've been awake longer than I have," Joanne said.

"It's been a long day for both of us."

"The forest is an interesting place, isn't it? It's too bad we aren't here just to explore."

He shook his head. Nothing could crush her. She had always been the one who pointed out something unusual when they went on their walks across the plateau. The most commonplace animal behavior could evoke excited comments from her. She had been studying linguistics, but in many ways she had a much more natural interest in the biological world than he did. He was interested in theories and practical uses, whereas she was simply amused and awed by what she observed.

It irritated him a little to hear her speak so lightly. He

had been looking at things all this while with the grim eyes
of a hunted animal. Still, what good did it do to concentrate on your fear and your loss? He should be irritated
with himself. She was keeping her eyes open and her spir-
its up and that was important if they wanted to survive.

"Maybe we'll come back and explore it," he said.

"We might as well." She chuckled nervously. "It looks
like we're going to have plenty of time."

The chuckle was a good sign she was tired.

In his early teens—he had been twelve when they had
landed on the plateau—he had often stood at the edge
of the cliff and thought about exploring the forest. He and
his father had had several violent arguments about it. For a
long time he had thought his father was a coward—or a
tyrant who wanted to keep the people in the settlement
penned up on the plateau so he could boss everyone
around. Once he had even dreamed about running away
and spending his life studying this new world and making
astonishing discoveries; he would have to live without wom-
en, of course, and without any food other than a cheese
fungus, but it would be a heroic existence which would
be remembered forever in the legends of mankind.

Swallowing the last of his cheese fungus, he denounced
his youthful self for a fool. The taste of the stuff was always unpredictable and rarely good. Despite the hopes
of the genetic engineers who had developed it, it resembled
a cheese only in its consistency and its yellowish color.

The planners of the proposed interstellar expedition had
assumed, correctly, that the plant and animal life of a habitable planet might resemble Earth life in many superficial ways
but that its chemical structure would be different enough to
make it inedible. The cheese fungus had been developed to
provide a safe food until Earth plants and animals could
be grown in abundance. In effect it was a biological chemi-

cal plant which attacked the local plant life thrown into its bed, broke the local proteins down into their elemental chemicals, and reassembled the elements into proteins humans could digest.

He washed the taste out of his mouth with a swig of water from his canteen. Reaching behind him, he patted her hand. "We can camp here if you want to."

"I'm all right. Am I slowing you up too much? You could probably walk twice as fast without me."

"Without you I probably wouldn't be here."

She leaned backward so she could look at his face. "Then I'm glad I came. Wouldn't you have left without me?"

He shook his head.

"We can make some kind of life, Harold. There really is a lot of work you can do here. I feel as bad as you, but we've got to go on."

He kissed her lips. He knew he should be watching the trees, but he couldn't help it. Her concern for him demanded a response.

He held her face between his hands and looked at her. He had never seen so much tenderness in a woman's eyes.

"I guess on Earth they would have called this a honeymoon," he said.

"I'll try to be a good wife to you. I promise."

"I was going to ask you sooner or later anyway."

A dark blur sped at him through the fog. He grabbed his club and scrambled to his feet. Joanne gasped and he jerked his head around. Two almost invisible shadows were rushing at them from the front of the cart. Three more were coming at them from the back. A sixth was charging straight at Joanne.

"*Get up!*"

His eyes darted from side to side. Behind him Joanne stood

up clumsily. The waterproof boxes piled in the cart made a rickety, uneven platform.

He shook the club. The animal coming at him from the front was only about ten meters away. The others were almost as close. They were as silent as the fog. If they hadn't been moving, he would never have noticed them.

He hadn't thought about animals which hunted in packs. There were too many for the bow and too many for the club.

"Kill them!" he bawled. "Don't be squeamish!"

A solid looking body leaped at him from the right. He twisted on his hips and the club smashed into a round skull. A solid impact jarred his arms. The animal screamed. He twisted with it as it hurtled past and slammed the club into the flank of the thing leaping at him from the left.

Nails slid into flesh and ribs. Claws tore at the loose folds of his shirt. Joanne yelled and fell over the side of the cart.

He fought for his balance. On the ground below the beast he had first seen charging him was crouching to spring. Bending his knees, he leaped over the side after Joanne.

One of the creatures had pounced on her as soon as she fell. He yelled savagely. Oblivious of everything except the claws and teeth threatening her face, he brought the club down on the beast's back.

Bone crunched. The spine snapped and the animal screamed and thrashed. Claws raked on Joanne's clothes. Hands over her face, she struggled to roll out from under.

Two of the animals were crouching an easy leap away. He snarled at them and raised the club over his head with one hand. Grabbing the broken-backed creature by the neck, he wrenched it off Joanne.

"Get up!"

He glared at the two crouching beasts. At his feet the one with the broken back coughed out its life. The animal he had stabbed in the side glared at him from the ground and yapped.

Joanne pulled herself up the side of the cart. The fourth beast stalked around the front end and crouched beside the one which had been wounded in the side.

"Pick up your club," Harold said.

She picked up her club. "Are you hurt?"

"Not yet." Orange eyes stared at him through the mist. *Why didn't they jump?* "How are you?"

"I don't feel any blood."

"Why don't they do something?"

One of the crouching animals yapped several times. Harold's hand tightened on the club. Three against two. If Joanne could hold her own, they might get out of this.

The wounded animal barked once. The other animal yapped again. The wounded animal barked and moved its head.

"Harold . . ."

"Do you think you can use the bow?"

"I think they're talking."

He blinked. His eyes passed from round head to round head.

They had bodies a little like the bodies of cats, lithe and big pawed, but their faces were almost as flat as a human's, and their teeth looked shorter and duller than a carivore's teeth should. They hadn't run at an impressive pace when they attacked either. Even hunting in packs, if their teeth and claws and that speed were all they had to work with, they couldn't be very efficient killers. Unless they weren't as well fed as they appeared to be, they had to have some weapon that didn't show.

They were crouching around him and Joanne exactly like a gang of humans who were afraid to move in because nobody wanted to be the first one hurt—like creatures who could size up a situation and predict what would happen if they acted.

For the first time in history, humans were face to face with an alien intelligence.

For a moment, in spite of the danger, he felt some of the excitement of discovery. He had imagined this moment many times as he looked down on the forest from the plateau. What insights two entirely different species could give each other! His father had insisted any intelligent beings who lived on this world had to be at a low level culturally, but there had always been the possibility the natives were masters of some other skill, such as social organization, or that they had created a technology so simple and efficient humans couldn't recognize it. They might even know how the human race could control the follies which had wrecked civilization on Earth.

An idea flashed across his mind. Theorists had often argued that human hands had triggered the development of human intelligence. Man was supposed to have evolved from an animal which had used primitive tools and weapons when it hunted. Tools had created a way of life, and the way of life had made tools more and more necessary. Instead of favoring the strong and the fast, natural selection had begun to favor the intelligent, the people who could use tools with more skill and imagination than the rest of the pack. Here was some evidence for that theory! If Joanne were right, these creatures had a language but no hands. If they had evolved from some animal which had hunted in packs, and which had used primitive signals to coordinate the hunt, then on this world, too, intelligence had evolved because a species had become dependent on a skill only intelligence could improve.

He cursed. "What difference does it make? They attacked us! For all we know they're just savages." He loosened his knife in its sheath. The excitement had lasted only an instant. They might be intelligent, but they were no more civilized than the intelligent animals he had left behind on the plateau. "Get the bow. Climb on the cart and shoot the one standing by the one lying on the ground. I can take the other two. They can't know what the bow is. They don't have any hands."

"What if they want to be friends?"

"They can leave. Who's stopping them?"

One of the crouching animals grunted. The wounded animal barked again.

Joanne's hand flew to her mouth. "They can't leave the one that's wounded! That's what it is! They can't leave and they're afraid to attack us. Why don't we back away and see if they'll leave?"

"We can't leave our food here unprotected."

"The cheese fungus is on the back of the cart. I can pick up the box as we back up. We can't kill them, Harold. They may be trying to get out of this, too."

"Then why did they attack us?"

"They probably thought we were just a new kind of animal."

He shook his head. He was letting his anger get out of hand again. He wanted to live but he wasn't blind to the long-term implications. Sooner or later the humans in the settlement were going to have to start living on the same world with these people.

"Start backing up."

She edged along the side of the cart. Four heads followed her. He felt as if he were staring at a drawn bow.

She picked up the waterproof box at the end of the cart and he started backing away with her. He wanted to pick up his bow but he didn't dare make any mysterious moves. If he had seen one of them do something he didn't understand, he would have assumed the worst and attacked.

He stopped about twenty paces from the cart. "Lower your club. Let's see what happens."

They rested on their clubs. He thought about yelling to them—perhaps his tone of voice would communicate something—and then he decided anything he did would probably be misunderstood. The message was now as clear as they could hope to make it.

Humans and—what?—stared at each other. The four shadows by the cart were so still that at this distance he wouldn't have seen them if he hadn't known they were there.

"It's a good thing they don't know how tired I am," he said. "If they did, they wouldn't have hesitated."

Joanne chuckled. "It's a good thing they don't know how I fight."

The wounded one barked several times.

"What are they doing?" Harold murmured. "I can hardly see them."

"Two of them just ran away. I can't see them anymore."

"Watch my back."

"Here they come. It looks like they're dragging something between their teeth."

He peered into the darkness. They seemed to be gathered into a dark shadow where the wounded one was lying. There was a lot of low barking and yapping, like murmured conversation, and then the shadow seemed to break up.

Joanne gasped. "It's a stretcher! They're dragging him away!"

"It looks like you were right."

"God help us."

He put his arm around her shoulder and pressed her

face against his chest. His head moved from side to side as he checked to make sure they weren't being attacked again. He felt exhausted. Every time he turned around something new happened.

They trudged back to the cart. He picked up his bow and stared at the two corpses.

"We'd better keep going. They'll be back after these."

She lifted her cart handle. "Are you as tired as I am?"

"All I want to do is get someplace where I can lie down and stop feeling. Try to keep alert. We'll try to walk another hour."

They heaved and the cart rolled out of the depressions it had made in the ground. Around him the forest and the darkness looked more menacing than ever. He wondered how many of these creatures there were and when they would be back—and at the same time the scientist in him, the eternally curious human, wondered about their way of life, and how they had managed to build those statues and towers if they didn't have hands.

III

STANDING ON the lowest brach of a rough-barked black-tree, Eight Leader Nimenlej Lumin held himself semi-erect by clinging to an outcropping on the trunk with his left hand. He stared dumfoundedly at the Itiji hanging in the net. The spearman crouching beside him on the branch snorted derisively.

"You want my word!" His voice rose with anger and surprise.

The Itiji's orange eyes stared back at him. It had been hanging in the net since morning while Nimenlej and his Eight rounded up the rest of its pack. It obviously needed water and relief from the insects attacking the wound in its hind leg, but it hadn't whimpered once in all those hours. Even when its mate and its youngest children had called to it from the nearby nets in which they were now confined, the orange eyes had revealed only a momentary flicker of emotion and the powerful jaws had remained shut.

And then, unexpectedly, the Itiji had called its guard and asked to see the chief of its captors, claiming it had information the city of Imeten would want to hear.

"I know the people of your city," the Itiji said. "You keep your word." It spoke the language of Imeten fluently, even though the words had been shaped by a different tongue.

"I keep my word to my own people," Nimenlej said. He glanced at the spearman. "To my equals."

"If you won't keep your word to me, you won't give it. You are a Warrior of Imeten."

All his training told him he should have the Itiji killed on the spot. It was assuming he would feel obligated to treat it as an equal. And wasn't that equivalent to implying he might think he was as low in the scheme of things as it was?

Only one thing kept his hand from the stubby spear which protruded from the sheath on his back. He had been fighting the Itiji for six years now, since his seventeenth birthday, and unlike some of the priests and politicians who stayed in the safe shelter of the city, lecturing about a world in which everything had been created to serve their own well-served selves, he had come to respect the courage and

shrewdness of the creatures he fought. He captured them and
took them home to be slaves, but they were no lower in
his eyes than the slaves of his own species. Anyone could
become a slave. It was easy for a priest like Telmuj Elt Mujin
to say a truly brave man would die rather than be a slave,
and, therefore, anyone who submitted to slavery deserved to
be a slave, but those who had faced brave, determined enemies in battle knew the gods had rules the priests had
never heard of. The bravest warrior who had ever lived
had been afraid many times, and could be forced to surrender if his enemies caught him at the right time, and
it was the will of the gods. Didn't even the legends of
his own city tell how the founder himself, Jinel Tun Teljul,
had panicked and cursed the goddess Niluji when his enemies had him trapped on a burning branch?

He might become a slave himself one day, if Lidris of
Drovil ever attacked Imeten. He hoped he would die first,
taking many brave men with him, but who knew what
he would do if he ever found himself surrounded and
disarmed?

"Even if I keep my word," he said, "even if I let your
son free, how do you know I won't capture him again tomorrow?"

The Itiji closed its eyes. "Give him the night to escape.
After that—it's the will of the gods."

"Will you swear you won't try to escape while we're going back to Imeten?"

"Don't ask for too much. What I have to tell you is
worth my son to you."

"You can't escape anyway. It will be an easier trip for
all of us if you don't try."

The Itiji stared past him. By now he knew them well
enough to understand some of the emotion in its eyes. It
was thinking of the forest where it would never run again,

29

and it was thinking of the road from the iron mine on which most of the Itiji slaves dragged huge sleds to Imeten. Or would they blind it and put it to work hauling water to the baths?

He rarely visited the mines. He always thought of the Itiji as he knew them in the forest, as brave, fierce warriors who tested his courage and his cunning. What happened to them after they were captured was as shadowy in his thoughts as what happened to mortals after death.

"I'll swear," the Itiji said. "For my son. What choice do I have?"

"Then I give you my word." He unhooked his mace from his belt and held it over his head. "I swear by the goddess Niluji and by my courage as a Warrior. If you tell me information which I know in my stomach is of value, your eldest son will go free—and he may have until sundown tomorrow to run as far from my nets as he can."

"By my name," the Itiji said, "and by the name of my father, and by the gods who dwell in the mountains, I will not try to escape until we reach Imeten."

He returned the mace to his belt. "Now what do you have to tell?"

"Twelve days ago, creatures we had never seen before entered our land, dragging a kind of sled we had never seen before. At first in the darkness we thought they were some of your people. We followed them and I and my sons attacked them." The Itiji paused. "They were not of your people. They look like you but they walk on their hind legs without holding on to anything. They have hands like you, but they live on the ground like us." It paused again. "They can use their hands all the time, even when they're walking."

Nimenlej kept his face under control. The inferior beside him must not see how he felt.

The fierce pleasure in the Itiji's eyes was unmistakable. It had won its son's freedom, but it had also achieved something which must taste almost as sweet: revenge for its own enslavement.

It had to be lying! How merciless could the gods be!

"How many were there?"

"Two," the Itiji said.

"Did you see any others?"

"We didn't look. They fought us off with clubs."

"Where are they now?"

"They've made a camp on the edge of the mountains."

"How far?"

"For us it would be a day and a morning's walk."

"Would they still be there if I went looking for them?"

"If they weren't, you could probably follow the tracks their sled makes."

The Itiji's flat, subtly mocking tone compelled belief. What had the gods sent against him? If slaves had not been desperately needed by the city, if he had not been promised a wife from Jemil Min Mujin's own collection if he brought back eight Itiji, oath or no oath he would have dropped on the net then and there and caved in its skull with his mace.

Beside him, emotion finally overcame discipline. The spearman, who had been so contemptuous only a moment ago, rolled forward onto his knees and swayed back and forth on the branch with his face staring at the ground.

"The gods of the mountain! The gods themselves!"

Nimenlej dropped to all fours. His right fist shot into the grovelling insect's skull.

"Silence! Get back on your haunches!"

The spearman shook his dazed head. His big shoulders rocked back and forth. He looked up at his leader and his right hand shot toward his spear.

Nimenlej reached behind his shoulder and jerked his own spear out of its sheath. The spearman froze with his fingers gripping the shaft of his weapon.

They stared at each other. "Get on your haunches," Nimenlej whispered. "Get up or I'll have you hanging in a net, too."

On neighboring branches the rest of his men turned to watch. They had all seen incidents like this many times. If he ever wavered they would be on him in an instant. They obeyed him only because they feared him, and because they knew that if they killed a Warrior of Imeten they would be hunted through the forest like Itiji by the lords of every city.

The spearman took his hand off his spear. Scowling at the captive Itiji, he resumed his proper stance.

"That's better," Nimenlej said.

He stared at the man thoughtfully, as if he were inspecting his posture or planning his punishment. Was the Itiji lying? This could be a trap. To investigate the story he would have to leave slaves lightly guarded in the wilderness, where his men might be attacked at any time by Itiji or other slavers. He was as disturbed as the fool crouching before him, but that was no excuse for stupidity.

On the other hand, the Itiji knew enough about Imeten to understand exactly what would happen to him if he were lying.

Who knew what the gods had created in the lands beyond the mountains, or on the other side of the ocean? Suppose he returned to Imeten with a new kind of slave? Powerful new allies? Suppose it really were the gods themselves. Why not pray to them in person? Imeten could use some help.

If he went back to Imeten now and told the story, they would mock him for a fool for believing the word of an Itiji. If he wanted anyone important to believe him, he at least had to be able to say he had seen the things with his own eyes.

He roared for his second in command. "Tun!"

Crouching on the branch just above the Itiji's net, Ilnjet Tun Tinjun had been watching the scene with glittering eyes. Now he slapped the wood and bowed his head.

"My lord!"

"I'm going to the mountains with two men. I'm leaving you and four men here with the slaves. Four days in the nets and they'll be worthless. Make sure you feed them, too. If anything happens to them or the men while I'm away, you're responsible."

He pushed his spear into its sheath. Resting on his right arm, he pointed his left hand at the Itiji. "You'll come with me. Your son stays here until we come back."

The Itiji glanced at the other nets. It moaned something it its own tongue and then it threw back its head and howled its anguish at the treetops.

Its mate and two of its sons joined its protest. Nimenlej listened stonily. He had heard similar outcries many times. Sooner or later they always started wailing. This one had lasted longer than most, but basically they had less self-control than most children.

Their complaint made a strange, throbbing music. He had never told anyone but he liked to hear Itiji sing. Sometimes he would creep up on a group in the forest and delay the ambush for a long time because he was listening to their music. He had lost at least two good lots that way.

· The howls died away. "Lower the net, Tun. Release it. Dartblowers—point your weapons at the other nets. Kill them if it tries to escape."

The Itiji's mate barked at it. He knew enough of their language to gather she was telling it to run away anyway. Apparently she had little respect for the oath of a warrior.

The two dartblowers in the Eight aimed their tubes at the other nets. Tun and another man hung their weight on the rope which held the Itiji's net, and which had been passed over the branch above them and tied to the branch on which they were standing. When they had enough slack, Tun reached down with one hand and untied the knots. Their muscles bulged as they fought to keep the net from dropping too fast. They knew how to treat the property of their betters.

They let go as soon as the Itiji's paws touched the ground. The net fell away from its captive and the Itiji arched its back and stretched.

"You can put your weapons down," the Itiji shouted. "You have my son and my oath. If it weren't for that, I'd let us all die."

Nimenlej grabbed the trunk and pulled himself semi-erect. Far below, a huge moth fluttered between him and the Itiji. "You're going to lead us to these new animals you've discovered. I hope we find them. If we don't sight them in two days, you and your family will wish you had died."

He picked two men for the journey and inspected their weapons and their equipment. After a little thought he reduced the food supply to one loaf per man, a skimpy ration for a four to five day hike, and told the spearman to hook two extra spears on his back and the dartblower to triple the number of darts he carried. They could live off the trees. They might need all the weapons they could carry.

He thought about using the Itiji for a pack animal and then decided against it. The idea offended him and he knew enough about slave handling to know this one would have to be broken in by a veteran.

"I don't know if the Itiji is lying or not," he told the two men who were going with him. "If it is, it's going to wish it hadn't. If it's telling the truth, every punishment for disobedience is doubled the instant we sight these things. Do what you're told and there'll be a feast for all of us as soon as we're home. The gods may be sending us a great gift. There may be some gifts from the High Warrior himself when we reach Imeten."

He looked down between his feet. Tun was already leading the pit-digging party hand over hand down the ropes they had hung from the lower branches. His second in command knew what to do when the Eight Leader was watching.

"Itiji!"

The Itiji looked up. It opened its mouth and then it closed it again—what could it answer that wasn't servile?—and waited for its orders.

"I will set the pace. You will stay just behind me and let me know at once if I stray from the right course. Do you understand?"

"I understand."

He turned to the two men who were going with him. "We'll have to stay closer to the ground than usual. Stay behind him and keep your eyes on him." He glanced at the dartblower. "If he tries to run, paralyze him."

He cupped his hand over his mouth. "We're ready, Itiji. Follow me!"

He leaped for the next highest branch, two long body lengths away. For a moment, arms and legs outstretched, he hung joyously weightless in the air. Far below, the Itiji's eyes followed him. Tun and the others looked up from where they were collecting wood and stones to make shovels.

His hands clutched the branch. He swung himself up and trotted along semi-erect, supporting himself by running his hand along the branch just above. At this level, and on up to where the top of the green canopy swayed beneath the sun, the branches were close enough together so that he could move comfortably.

The moisture from the leaves wet his face. His eyes darted from side to side and up and down, watching the Itiji and searching for birds and poisonous snakes and insects. Behind him his men padded silently after him. Unlike some of the people of Imeten, he and his men were not so far removed from the wilderness they couldn't be at ease where no bridges and hand-rails connected the trees.

The branch began to sway under his weight. He leaped three body lengths for a slightly higher branch on the next tree. His long arms reached for moist, fungus-covered wood. He swung along hand over hand and then pulled himself up and trotted on.

Birds and small animals scrambled out of his way. He slipped into the comfortable rhythm of the march and his mind began to calculate some of the things he might gain from this venture. At the very least, he would get a few extra days away from the city.

Soon the wailing of the enslaved Itiji was lost in the distance.

IV

HE STRUGGLED upward through a fitful sleep. The first morning light was beating on his eyes through the thin curtain he had hung across the entrance to their inflatable shelter. In the distance he could hear the squawks of the birds and animals in the trees.

He rolled over and propped himself on his elbow. Joanne was smiling in her sleep. He loved the way her pale skin looked in the morning light.

He picked up his club and crawled out of the shelter. Shrubbery and grass wet his legs as he walked down the hill swinging the canvas bucket. They were high enough above sea level that the tree line ended a good hundred meters below the hollow which hid their shelter from any passing eyes. A cliff guarded their back and the trench he had dug around the hollow reinforced the protection they got from the open space on their front and sides.

They had been here thirty days now. They had stopped as soon as they had found a place where they would have water and where he felt they could defend themeselves against a surprise attack. They would have been safer in the mountains but this had been as far as he could go. It had taken all his will to get them this far.

From his reading he knew the name for what he had been doing all this time. Freud had called it the mourning process, and it was the same whether you lost a leg, or a friend, or a way of life. The mind had to put together a new picture of the world, and for most people this meant a period of listlessness and depression while they concentrated on the job.

He was beginning to function again. For the last few days he had been more engrossed in the beauties and pleasures he shared with Joanne than in the catastrophe he had left behind in the settlement. He was a basically optimistic person. He could tolerate almost anything as long as he had work to do or as long as he could struggle. Defeat could crush him but not trouble.

He wasn't even sure they were going to go to the mountains. He wanted to know more about the creatures who had attacked them in the forest. Now that they had been forced to leave the plateau, why not make something good out of a bad situation? That first encounter could have been worse. Thanks to Joanne, he had shown them he didn't mean any harm—and they had shown him they were people who looked after their wounded.

He wasn't going to waste his life sitting around the first planet men had ever explored eating cheese fungus and growing rabbits. If he couldn't make his exile a major event in human history, he wasn't fit to be a man.

He dipped the bucket in the stream and started back up the hill. His body felt terrible. His beard itched and the salt in his sweat burned under his armpits. He would probably have to send Joanne after a second bucket before he got dressed again.

As he climbed out of the trench, something screamed behind him.

He put down the bucket and dropped into the hollow. His hand tightened on the club as he peered over the rim.

His heart jumped. Several four-legged creatures were crouching in the grass a few paces up the slope from the stream.

"What is it?" Joanne asked.

He glanced over his shoulder. She was standing in front of the door, with her hand over a yawn.

"Get your club."

She ducked into the shelter. One of the creatures screamed again. He raised his head cautiously. Joanne dropped down beside him and looked for herself.

She gasped. "Look at the trees."

He shielded his eyes from the sun. The shadows under the trees were a dark blur speckled with sunlight.

"Tell me what you see."

She didn't answer. When he looked at her she was shaking her head.

"Two of them, Harold. Two of them!"

"Tell me what you see!"

She closed her eyes. One of the creatures on the hill screamed and moved a couple of steps closer. He put his hand on her shoulder and waited patiently.

"Two of them are hanging from the vines under the trees," she said. "They've got tubes pointing at us—long tubes in front of their mouths like blowguns. They're all wearing clothes. The ones on the ground are squatting like gorillas or monkeys, but they're thinner and they've got hairless faces."

He peered desperately into the shadows. He was just as stunned as she was.

"They've all got stuff on their backs. I think they've got sheaths. It looks like they've got arrows in them. One of them has something in his belt. Their faces are long and thin with big foreheads and pointed ears."

"Do you see any more in the trees?"

"I think I can see metal flashing."

His bow was in the shelter. He knew almost nothing about the blowguns primitives had used on Earth, but if they had something that might be a blowgun pointed at him, he had better assume he was in range.

He stood up. He put the club on the ground and held out his hands palm upward.

One of the creatures on the ground jabbered rapidly. The entire group started shambling up the hill on all fours. The one in the lead seemed to be the one with something hanging on his belt.

"They look like they're clumsy on the ground," he said. "If it comes to a fight, I think we should try to run for it.

39

Go stand near the door. If we have to fight, I'll try to hold them off while you get the bow out of the shelter."

"What about the blowguns?"

"We won't fight unless we have to."

He had hidden a cache of supplies in a rock formation near the hollow. If they had to abandon what they had here, they could slip back after and pick it up. He had even included a pair of rabbits with enough food and water in their cage to keep them alive several days.

The creatures paused a few paces beyond the ditch. For the second time in thirty days he looked into the eyes of an intelligent being who had been shaped by the stresses and opportunities of another world.

If the creatures had been standing erect, they would have been about a head shorter than a human. Standing as they were, hands resting on the ground with their knees bent and their thick torsos leaning forward from the waist, their heads were about the height of his stomach.

They had three fingers and a thumb on each hand. The thing on the leader's belt looked like a well made mace. The equipment on their backs looked like it had been made with tools also. Since he didn't see any bows, he assumed the metal-pointed stakes sticking out of the sheaths on their back were probably spears. The leader and two others seemed to have short metal swords.

The leader screamed several syllables. His shoulders and hips wiggled as he talked as if he were doing some kind of dance. He clapped his head several times and Harold realized he was making the same sound over and over—neemenlej, neemenlej.

He glanced back at Joanne, who had stood up and moved back a couple of paces. "That must be his name. What do you think?"

"That's as good a guess as any. Tell him your name and see what he does."

He pointed at his chest. "Harold. Ha . . . rold. Haa . . . rold." He resisted the impulse to shout. To make it clear he was naming, he pointed at Joanne. "Joanne. Jo . . . anne." He clapped his head several times. "Harold. Harold."

"I hope you haven't just given me away," Joanne said.

The leader took one hand off the ground and pointed at his face. "Nimenlej. Ni . . . men . . . lej." He pointed at his followers. "Imeten. Imeten."

"I think you can assume he's named Nimenlej," Joanne said. "I can think of at least six things Imeten could mean."

Nimenlej shuffled around on all fours until his right side was facing the hollow. Her jerked his head and shoulders at the forest and screamed several syllables.

Harold frowned. "He could just be telling us where they're from." He rubbed his beard with his palm. "We'll pack the cart and start toward the mountains. If they stop us, we'll go with them and try to get away tonight."

"Shall I get the cart?"

"Right."

She disappeared behind the shelter. Their visitors stretched their necks so they could see into the hollow. When she came back dragging the cart, the entire group started jabbering. The leader shrieked and they shut up as if he'd turned off a switch.

They deflated the shelter and Joanne folded it neatly and packed their equipment while Harold rolled out the two logs he had cut for this purpose and laid them across the trench. Their visitors watched them intently. Every time Joanne put something new in the cart, they wiggled excitedly.

He packed the bow where he could get at it easily. He didn't try to hide it; he was certain they didn't know what it was.

"Are you sure you don't want to go with them?" Joanne asked.

"Do you?"

"What will we do in the mountains?"

"We'll come back. I'm forcing myself to be cautious. I'd like to spy on them from a distance for awhile before we got too involved with them."

They lifted the handles of the cart. She smiled at him bravely. "We'll be all right," he said.

They dragged the cart across the logs. The leader shrieked and his men spread out through the grass in a wide semi-circle.

Harold glanced at the trees. "Are the blowguns still there?"

"Yes."

He wondered what they thought he was. Would they kill him for a specimen if they thought they couldn't capture him alive?

He pointed at the grass-covered mountain peaks with his free hand. "I'm sorry we've been trespassing. We're on our way to the mountains. It's been a pleasure meeting you."

The leader shrieked as they took their third step. Screaming and shrugging at the forest, two of the creatures shuffled hurriedly into their path.

## V

ONCE THEY HAD grabbed vines and climbed hand over hand into the trees, their captors lost all their awkward-ness. They trotted along the lower branches and jumped across the open spaces from handhold to handhold as easily and gracefully as birds fly or fish swim. Just as man had evolved on the edges of the forest, a walking, weapon-using hunter with his pelvis and spine modified so he could stand erect with free hands and see for long distances, they had evolved, on this world covered with forest, in the trees themselves—and kept the tree-adapted anatomy which made them as awkward on the ground as a man would have been in the trees.

He watched them with such pleasure and wonder that he had trouble remembering he should be spying out their weaknesses and planning their escape. Two intelligent species . . .

Visions of a galaxy bursting with life crowded his head. Life must flower more vigorously than men had dared to imagine. What kind of creatures might be living on worlds as different from Earth as Jupiter and Mercury had been? How many unimaginable and varied civilizations had they passed as they cruised through the star systems in which they had failed to find planets men could inhabit?

Joanne stumbled and he jerked out of his revery. "Are you all right?"

"A rock turned under me."

"Is your ankle all right?"

"I think so. It doesn't hurt."

She was getting tired. Her face was covered with a thin film of sweat and the strain on his left shoulder told him he was pulling a bigger share of the load.

He looked up. Ahead of them the line of tree-dwellers on their left side was leaping across a gap between two trees. On the lowest branches on each side of them a blowgunner was trotting a few paces behind the cart. Two men armed with spears were trotting just ahead.

The line jumping the gap was well ahead of their immediate guards. Trotting seemed to be the natural pace of the tree-dwellers. They moved in spurts. They had rested twice already, both times after two kilometer dashes, and at least once during each hiking period the main party had crept far enough ahead that Nimelej had been forced to scream a halt so the humans could catch up.

"We should be stopping to rest soon," Harold said. "We'll have one advantage tonight—if we can keep away from them for the first two kilometers, we should be out of their hands for good. They're faster than us over any two kilometers, but we can do more kilometers per day."

"You're still planning to escape tonight? You're sure you don't want to spend a couple of more days with them?"

"We can't take the risk. The further we are from the cache, the longer we'll have to walk without supplies. We're going to have to leave everything behind but the weapons, some cheese fungus, and our canteens."

"I'm going to miss the shelter. It was our first home."

"I'll make you something better."

At night the tree-dwellers made a camp in the trees which completely encircled the cart. Directed by screams and a few blows from Nimenlej, they lit two fires on the lower branches and roasted the birds, fruit and animals they had foraged during the march. The evening light and his own bad eyes defeated Harold's attempts to determine the technique they used to start the fire.

Nimenlej offered them food several times before he accepted their refusal. They ate their cheese fungus surrounded by the odors of a feast. Harold's mouth watered every time the rabbits attracted his attention. He had thought about butchering them and reluctantly decided against it; if they didn't get away tonight, he would want something more than cheese fungus and vegetables when they reached wherever they were going.

After supper their hosts played games from a while. A contest in which two men tried to push each other off and of the upper branches seemed to be a big favorite with everybody. When the loser fell toward the ground, banging against branches and clutching desperately for a handhold, the entire group made a loud screeching noise and slapped the wood with their hands. They screeched even louder when both men fell off the branch.

The fires stayed lit after the group went to sleep. Four guards squatted on the branches just above the cart.

They unfolded their sleeping bags under the cart. He wanted a position from which he could see all their guards.

"I'll time the first guard period," he whispered. "Try to get some sleep. We'll go just before the second time they change guards. The guards on watch should be getting sleepy about then."

"What about the blowguns? The fires are almost as bad as daylight."

"I only see one. Check and see if I'm right."

She peered out from under the cart as cautiously as she could. "It looks like one blowgun and three spears."

He glanced at her face. "I can eliminate the blowgun with my bow."

"Harold—"

"We have to get away, Jo."

"We don't even know they're unfriendly! They may think we're their guests!"

"Is that why they're keeping us guarded?"

"They're probably afraid of us. We don't know anything about them. This may be the only chance we'll ever have to make peace"

"The longer we stay with them, the harder it will be to

get away. We're probably heading for a settlement. What'll we do if they throw us in a prison?"

"Can't we just run?"

"And get a dart in our backs?"

A guard stirred in the trees. He put his hand on her shoulder and she closed her mouth.

A guard shrieked at the top of his lungs. Wood clattered on metal pans. The whole camp sprang awake. Long-armed shadows leaped through the trees in the firelight.

Ropes dropped from the branches. Nimenlej and most of his men climbed down hand over hand and ran toward the cart, screaming excitedly and jerking their heads at the trees.

Harold slid out from under the cart and stood up. Nimenlej slapped the ground several times and pointed at the trees. More ropes dropped from the lower branches. Awkward forms swarmed over the cart and started tying ropes to the axles and the wheels.

Joanne stumbled to her feet. A rope, dropped from the branch directly overhead, brushed against Harold's face. Nimenlej screamed and pointed at the trees.

Something rumbled in the distance. A hum like a flight of insects teased his ears. Nimenlej shrieked. His men jumped on the ropes and started hauling themselves up.

Harold scooped up the sleeping bags and threw them on the cart. "Get on the cart! Hurry!"

She climbed on top of the cart. He grabbed a rope and started climbing. On a branch far above, faces glowing in the firelight, a line of tree-dwellers hauled on the ropes. A voice screamed rhythmically. The cart lurched and rose swaying toward the branches. Joanne stretched out flat on top of their equipment and peered into the darkness.

Hundreds of small animals shot out of the darkness. The hum vibrated unrelentingly in his skull. Heaving backs covered the ground. A cloud of insects and small birds flitted past his face.

The humming and the tiny forms darting at his eyes unnerved him. He pressed his face against the back of his hands. His muscles strained under his weight. He closed his eyes and hauled himself up the rope.

He opened his eyes. He was above the insects. He pulled himself up smoothly and arrived at the lowest branch just behind the cart.

They perched uneasily on a branch and watched the herd uproot and trample everything in its path but the trees themselves. When the animals finally disappeared, the ropes stayed up. Apparently they were supposed to spend the night on the branch. From what he could see of the ground in the firelight it was a good idea.

They slept with their backs against the trunk of the tree and a rope tied around their waists. When they awoke in the morning they both had headaches and pains in their backs and legs.

By the end of the second marching period they were further from the mountains than they'd ever been. Harold felt gloomy and Joanne was so tired she stumbled over every bump. Once he shouted down her protests and made her walk unhindered while he pulled the cart himself for two kilometers.

They went on making jokes, however, and he went on observing their captors. He made notes in his head as if he were planning to report to a scientific conference back on Earth.

"I think we'd better escape tomorrow during the day," he said. "We're too tired to do it tonight, and if we wait until tomorrow night we'll be three days' march from the cache. And it looks like they've got better hearing than we do, too. If they can track us down, I'd like to be able to fight back—and with them in the trees, the bow is the only weapon we've got." He glanced at her. "We won't hurt them unless they try to stop us."

Her eyes glittered. "I knew you'd decide something like that."

"It's only because we can't go tonight," he said gruffly. "If we go during the day, I think we can arrange it so we'll be almost out of range when we start running."

The next time they stopped to rest he started getting the tree-dwellers used to the idea that humans like privacy when they eliminate their body wastes. They both walked a good twenty meters from the camp with half a dozen tired guards trailing after them. One of them made a trip every break that day. After every meal they filled their canteens with water from their twenty-liter waterbag and broke some cheese fungus off the main bed and stuffed it in their pockets.

They climbed into their sleeping bags while their hosts were still rough-housing in the trees. He squeezed her hand once and then fell asleep as if he'd been clubbed.

The morning light woke him up just as the camp started bustling. He propped himself on his elbow and watched his wife yawn.

She looked up and smiled. "Feel better?" he said.

"Uh-huh. How are you?"

He put his hands on her shoulders and buried himself in a kiss. The knowledge they might both be dead soon hovered in his consciousness.

Nimenlej started the march minutes after the camp awoke. The tree trunks were still damp and the foliage still glistened with moisture. The morning air smelled warm and slightly sweet.

"I wonder what Nimenlej will do with the rabbits," Joanne said. "I hope they don't poison themselves."

She started walking away from the cart as soon as they stopped for the first break. A guard stalked along a branch several paces behind her. Harold leaned against the cart and fingered his bow and his quiver.

The tree-dwellers were scattered over the lower branches of three trees. Most of them had already stretched out on their stomachs with their long arms dangling over the sides. Nimenlej was munching on a fruit he had speared with his sword. Two men armed with blowguns were crouching on the branch closest to the cart.

He picked up the bow and the quiver and whirled away from the cart. "Run!"

Joanne broke into a stumbling, lopsided run. Her guard screamed and scrambled along his branch after her.

Voices shrieked. Wood clattered on metal. He ran after Joanne's swaying back with his bow clutched in one hand and his quiver in the other. His overgrown thigh muscles resisted his every stride. He couldn't raise his knees high enough. His body had adapted to walking in this gravity, not to short distance running.

He looked back over his shoulder. Nimenlej was crouching on his branch, screaming orders and trying to shake the fruit off his sword. All over the camp men were rising to all fours. The two blowgunners were looking at Nimenlej with their weapons half raised, as if they were waiting for orders.

He looked up and smiled cheerfully and waved with the hand holding the bow as he passed Joanne's guard. He tried to think of some clever remark to cheer her up, but he found that his wit failed him. Although the guard screamed at him, he didn't reach for his weapons.

He slid the quiver over his shoulder and ran along behind her. When he looked back, Nimenlej and the rest of the main party were moving sluggishly along the branches. He had timed the thing perfectly. They looked like they were straining more than he was. After one of their two kilometer spurts they were just as tired temporarily as a human who had walked five times as far. If he had been running by himself, he could have gotten away easily.

"Run faster," he said. "It's only for a sprint. If we can stay ahead a kilometer, we'll wear them out."

"I'm doing my best."

She was panting already. She could hardly talk.

He looked back. They had moved into the upper branches. He could only see one or two dim shapes on the lower levels. He could judge where the others were only by their screams and by the noise of the birds and animals they disturbed.

He slapped a tree. "Thirty meters to the next one. Ten trees and we've won. C'mon."

He looked up. Far above, at the height where the sunlight speckled the leaves, two silhouettes jumped a gap almost directly overhead.

He pulled up beside her. "They're catching up with us. Hurry."

She lengthened her stride. Her face twisted as if she were in pain.

He looked up again. He couldn't see the two silhouettes. When he looked back he thought he could see several others creeping up on them. Their fur and their clothes blended with the shadows in the leaves. They would have been invisible if they had been standing still.

Joanne sobbed. "I can't keep it up."

"You've got to."

"Go on without me."

"Don't be ridiculous."

She stumbled. He grabbed her elbow and held her

on her feet. Wild screams above and behind told him the tree-dwellers were gaining.

They should have escaped at night. She was too slow. He had let her make him soft-hearted.

"*Run!*"

She stumbled again. He grabbed at her but she slipped out of his grasp.

She landed on her knees. He stepped behind her and pulled her up by the shoulders. "Can you stand up?" They had run less than five hundred meters.

Something thumped against a tree. He looked up. A weighted rope had wrapped itself around a branch just ahead of them.

Another weight flew through the leaves and swung around the branch. *Thump. Thump.* Three screaming demons swung out of the trees.

Joanne stood up. The three tree-dwellers dropped in front of them on all fours and turned around. Crouching on three limbs, they jerked spears out of their sheaths and poised them above their heads.

He turned Joanne to the left. "Run!"

A voice shrieked. A spear streaked past her face.

He whirled, his hand leaping to his quiver. An arrow slammed into the shoulder of a spearman. The third spearman screamed and hurled his shaft.

He dropped to the ground and the spear flew over his back. The two spearmen who could still run turned tail and fled toward the nearest tree.

*Thump. Thump. Thump.*

He looked back as he jumped to his feet. A dark body was swinging at him like a cannonball.

He jumped to one side. Three more screaming bodies swung at him simultaneously. A long kick slammed into his

51

chest and knocked him off his feet. A hand wrenched the bow from his grasp.

Joanne screamed. He looked up from the dirt and saw a weighted net fall on her from the trees.

He stood up. His head felt dizzy. He pulled out his knife and ran toward her.

Ropes dropped from the trees above the net. Two blow-gunners slid out of the branches and hung by one hand with their tubes at their mouths. More weighted ropes were thumping on the branches. The men who had taken his bow were all crouching on the ground with spears poised above their heads.

He put the knife in its sheath. Joanne stopped struggling. He raised his hands above his head and hoped they understood what he meant.

## VI

THEY KEPT Harold's bow and arrows and confiscated his knife. Two guards rode the cart all day. When they stopped at night Nimenlej had the cart and their sleeping bags encircled by a cage made out of two nets pegged to the ground.

Every day was like the day before. The ground rose and fell and they passed small rivers and waterholes, but the forest was basically the same everywhere. Every day the sun filtered down to their eyes through the green canopy; birds and animals squawked in the trees and watched them from hiding; and they dragged the cart and its two passengers south while Nimenlej and his men trotted overhead.

Joanne blamed herself for the catastrophe. When she developed red, itchy spots on her hands and neck, Harold wondered if it was an allergic reaction or a guilt reaction. She had sensitive redhead's skin, however, and allergic reactions were the curse of human life on Delta Pavonis II; the difference in chemistry which protected them from parasites and germs meant they were surrounded by matter more foreign to their bodies than anything they could have touched or breathed on Earth. His mother had died from an allergy which had festered her lungs.

The fear that the allergy would spread to Joanne's face tormented them both more than any of the hardships of the march. They had both been astonished by the pleasure they had gotten from their bodies during the thirty days they had spent on the edge of the mountains.

"I couldn't stand it if something spoiled that, too," Joanne said one night. "As long as I know we can enjoy each other, I feel like I can stand up to anything that's waiting for us."

"You're a brave girl," Harold murmured.

"Are you glad I'm your wife?"

"You're the best wife I could have married."

The ground became rough as they approached the great river which meandered between the mountains and the southern ocean for thousands of miles before it finally turned sharply south. With tributaries flowing toward the river on either side, they were actually crossing a swamp in the forest. Something held them up at almost every lap. If they didn't have to haul the cart across ruts dug by swift creeks, or wade with it across a wide, shallow river, then they had to circle an immense fallen log or a thick clump of low brush while their captors cut straight across and let them catch up during the rest period.

They rested once for every two or three times the tree-dwellers rested. Harold didn't know whether Nimenlej was being cruel or just indifferent. He tried not to hate him. There might still be some hope that he and Joanne could establish a friendly relationship with these people.

Early one afternoon he looked up from the maze of damp, insect-infested shrubbery through which they had been picking their way for the last kilometer, and saw a sheet of daylight in front of him for the first time since they had left the hills. They were approaching the river.

The tree-dwellers stood on the lower branches and watched them drag the cart through the shrubbery. The full light of the sun blasted them in the face as they stepped out of the shade of the last row of trees.

They let go of the cart handles and shaded their eyes with their hands. Clouds of black insects hummed above the wide back of the river. Strange birds skimmed over the current. Ponderous animals wallowed near the banks. And on the opposite shore, above the dark wall formed by the trees, a high, wooden tower and a great, six-armed statue rose above the forest.

Nimenlej pointed. "Imeten. Imeten."

Harold rubbed his forehead wearily. "Tell me what you see," he said to Joanne.

"Some kind of wooden framework extends out of the trees to the shore. I can see tree-dwellers moving around on it. It looks like some of them are hauling things up from the river."

They were crossing on a raft which floated downstream from the opposite shore when Nimenlej signalled with a red flag. Nimenlej sat on top of the cart and most of his men crowded around him, holding on precariously. On the opposite shore someone pulled them across with a rope tied to an iron stake on the prow.

Joanne's face darkened. "Oh no."

"What's the matter?"

"We're being pulled by some of the creatures we met in the forest. They're being prodded with a pole by a tree-dweller."

Hundreds of screaming, chattering tree-dwellers crowded onto the grid-like framework as they approached. The raft bumped against the shore. Nimenlej and his men jumped onto the grid with drawn weapons and shoved the crowd back. They pulled the cart up the bank and dragged themselves under the shade of the trees, surrounded by noise and curious eyes.

They were obviously in—or under—a settlement. It looked like a big one. For Harold, in fact, it was the biggest settlement of intelligent beings he had ever seen in his life. He had seen movies of Earth's cities, but it still came as a shock. The clamor unnerved him. Noisy, wiggling bodies swarmed through the leaves in every direction. Bridges and handholds connected every tree. Huts covered with bark and leaves hung from branches, nestled in forks, and perched on platforms which looked as if they had been skillfully carpentered and properly braced against the trunks. Some trees were covered from the lowest branches to the highest with a spiral of dwelling places. With a planet-wide forest to live in, the tree-dwellers seemed determined to get as close to each other as they could.

They stopped before another wooden grid. Far above them—tiny figures against a patch of sky—a procession was descending hand over hand.

Nimenlej slid down a vine and crouched beside Joanne.

He screamed an order and his men slapped the branches they were standing on and drew their weapons.

A high pitched wind instrument shrieked twice. The crowd shut up so abruptly he and Joanne both started.

The procession halted just above their heads. The man in the center hung in the grid and observed them with little flickering eyes. He was about a head taller than the others and was flanked by two guards with drawn glowguns.

Nimenlej slapped the ground. The man in the grid screamed several syllables and Nimenlej started a long monologue.

Harold glanced at Joanne. She was listening carefully. The art of learning new lanuages had been highly developed on Earth during the last decade of the twentieth century, and she was one of several people in the settlement who had been encouraged to master it. Even during the worst part of the march she had managed to spend some time each day studying the screams of their captors. She already knew several words and two simple phrases.

Nimenlej slapped the ground. The man in the grid turned toward the humans and pointed at his chest with his thumb. "Jemil . . . Min . . . Mujin." He paused. "Jemil . . . Min . . . Mujin. Jemil . . . Min . . . Mujin"

He paused again. He unhooked the iron, obviously functional mace on his belt and raised it above his head. Solid blows crashed on the grid as he screamed a long harangue. Harold guessed he was making a ritual series of brags and titles. They might not know his language, but he wanted them to know he had more to say than his name when he introduced himself.

The harangue stopped abruptly. The mace described an arc which took in the entire city.

"Imeten . . . Imeten . . . Imeten . . ."

Harold pointed to his chest. "Harold Lizert. Harold . . . Lizert . . . Harold . . . Lizert . . ." He drew himself up.

He pointed at the sky and across the river at the mountains. "I am Harold the Magnificent," he shouted, "Ambassador High, Mighty and Terrible from the People Who Dwell in the Mountains, Man Among Men, Illustrious Descendant of Albert Einstein, William Shakespeare, Isaac Newton, Sigmund Freud, Socrates, Homer and Ulysses, He Who Comes From the Great Shining Land Beyond the Sky, Amen."

He glanced at Joanne. She was stifling a smile.

"Joanne Hamilton . . . Joanne Hamilton . . . Joanne . . . Hamilton . . . Wife of the Illustrious and Apparently Irrepressible Person Who Stands Beside Me."

Jemil Min Mujin screamed an order. Two spearmen descended from the trees with Harold's weapons. He looked them over without comment and turned his attention to the cart. Nimenlej shrugged at the wheels and jerked one of the handles with one hand.

Jemil Min Mujin screamed another harangue. Nimenlej slapped the ground. The wind instrument shrieked again and the procession turned around and ascended the grid.

The people in the crowd started talking again. Nimenlej shrugged at the cart. The humans picked up the handles and he led them further into the forest.

They stopped beside a trail, a narrow patch of worn ground which extended into the forest as far as Joanne could see. They were apparently on the edge of the city. Harold felt relieved when he realized there were no houses overhead; he had seen enough refuse on the ground to be worried about garbage and droppings.

Guards took up positions in the trees. Nimenlej screamed. In the upper reaches of the canopy an invisible party of workmen lowered a huge wooden tub filled with water.

For the first time in ten days they took a bath. The watching eyes made Joanne hesitate only a moment. She hated dirt and the tree-dwellers were not only not human—for all she knew they might not even be male.

They relaxed in the tub as if they had just come home from a trip. That night Harold could even look at the nets which caged them without boiling with frustration. Tomorrow they wouldn't have to walk. Tonight he could hold a clean woman in his arms. He would worry later.

The next morning a gang of carpenters began erecting a shelter on the lowest branch of a tree. Nimenlej arrived with a man dressed in a new kind of clothing—a shirt made of feathers, and a flat hat woven from vines—and their lessons began.

The language was not difficult. The Imetens even used the same subject-verb-object structure the Indo-European languages used. They classified things differently—they had dozens of words for the various states-of-being of plants, for example—but most of the novelties were either easy to understand or irrelevant for present puposes. The big problem was pronunciation. No human would ever be able to scream like an Imeten. He might learn to make himself understood, but he would always sound like an alien.

Twice, during the next few days, teams of the four-legged language speakers labored past their camp dragging sleds loaded with great mounds of iron ore. The teams were always surrounded by guards and they were always wailing mournfully.

Their enslavement outraged Joanne. She automatically sided with the oppressed. Harold felt compelled to warn her she mustn't let Nimenlej know her feelings. The Eight Leader called the fourlegs the Itiji, the "talking animals," and his contempt was obvious.

From what they had learned from their language lessons, slavery was a normal part of Imeten society. If they couldn't win more status than captives usually received, they might be in serious trouble.

They practised the language until their throats were hoarse. On the fourth day Nimenlej decided a trip through the city would be useful. Sixteen guards formed a cordon around them and they followed the Eight Leader up a ladder into the trees.

They spent most of the day clambering after Nimenlej on ladders and bridges thirty and forty meters above the ground. Joanne was in danger almost every step. Harold didn't know which was worse: watching her or looking down.

Everywhere they looked, curious faces peered at them from windows or out of shaded, hidden places in the leaves. Slaves with heavy packs trotted along on all fours and swung hand over hand across the undersides of bridges occupied by their betters. Warriors with maces on their belts savagely elbowed the lower classes out of their way. Common soldiers armed with spears maneuvered through the branches to the harsh commands of their leaders.

The slavery disgusted both of them. In the crowded workshops slaves forged tools and weapons. In the farms on top of the city, under the full heat of the sun, slaves cultivated vines and fruits and tended a herd of long, many legged, leaf-munching animals. In the baths near the great tower, Itiji slaves poured the buckets into a trough which emptied into a series of overflowing terraces—a series which ended far below with a crowd of slaves washing in the water dirtied by their masters.

The city resounded with screamed commands. Force and pain seemed to be the only social technique the Imetens knew. Nimenlej treated his Imeten subordinates, Harold noted, almost as roughly as he treated the slaves.

The baths were the worst part. As soon as he realized

the Itiji slaves had been blinded, Harold tried to turn Joanne away. He moved too late. He had to hold her against his chest and evade Nimenlej's questions while she fought to get herself under control.

A big, noisy crowd surrounded the central grid. Their guards cleared a path through it with drawn weapons, screaming orders and shoving anyone who didn't move out of the way fast enough.

"The High Warrior commands! Move! Move!"

In the center of the grid two men were climbing hand over hand toward the top. They seemed to be racing. They were facing each other across a single section of the grid and one man was one rung ahead.

Nimenlej turned to Harold. His shoulders wiggled with excitement. "The gods are speaking."

The man who was trailing jumped across the framework. His right hand closed around the rung his opponent was standing on. He jerked his mace off his belt and swung at the other man's legs.

Joanne turned her head. Harold put his hand on her shoulder and made himself watch.

The man on top twisted away from the blow. He let go with his hands and dropped on the other man's back. His legs gripped the other man's torso. He grabbed his opponent's wrist with one hand and pulled his mace off his belt with the other.

The man on the bottom screamed. He kicked away from the framework and the two bodies fell toward the ground. Wrestling and shrieking, they banged against the grid. A mace flashed in the sunlight. The crowd screamed.

A long arm grabbed at a rung. The two falling bodies broke apart. One clutched at the framework and the other fell silently toward the forest floor.

The victor pulled himself up the framework. Horns shrieked. Metal pans clattered. At the top of the grid a priest of the goddess Niluji raised his vine hat at the sky.

"The gods have spoken! Obey the gods!"

Nimenlej explained the custom as they made their way back to the camp. The Imetens believed the gods spoke through battle. They settled all disputes by battle, and they picked their government by battle, too. Once every year, when the two brightest stars were in the right position in the sky, all the seventeen-year-old boys in the city, except those who had chosen to be priests, fought in the grid until every man was either dead or a prisoner. The few who survived without yielding became Warriors for life. Those who would surrender rather than die became inferior soldiers. The custom had been handed down many generations before by the founder of the city, Jinel Tun Teljul, and according to Nimenlej it had made the Warriors of Imeten feared up and down the river.

"Every city envies us," Nimenlej screamed. "We have more slaves per free man than any city on the Great River. The bodies of our women torment the dreams of every male who had heard of Imeten."

That night Joanne had trouble sleeping. Twice Harold woke to find her staring through the ropes at the campfires and the mist.

He knew how she felt. He had read enough history to be aware that his ancestors had lived like the Imetens for thousands of years. Humans had groaned under slavery, too, and obeyed terrible customs, and killed and plundered so a few could enjoy the small surplus a primitive technology could wrest from the environment. To see the reality was another thing, however. He had decided the world was generally a cruel place, and that was the way of it, and a man had to live in it as best as he could, but even so, he found it hard to stay calm in the midst of so much suffering. And if it were almost too much for him, it must be a thousand times worse for Joanne.

"We'll get out of here somehow," he murmured.

"It won't make any difference," Joanne said. "They'll still be here. They'll still be living like this. And we'll know it."

A few days later Nimenlej escorted him into the city again. This time they went directly to the tower, the palace of the High Warrior himself, Jemil Min Mujin.

When they entered the assembly room, the High Warrior and his council of senior Warriors were all lying prone on the Imeten equivalents of chairs: padded, three-legged logs with chin-rests on one end. The senior Warriors reclined along both sides of the room and Jemil Min reclined alone at the front, a guard with a blowgun on each side. Even to Harold the room seemed cramped and crowded. The sweet smell of tree-dweller bodies stuffed his nostrils.

He stuck with the story he had given Nimenlej. He came, he claimed, from a people who lived in a land far to the north of the mountains. He had been forced to leave his city because of a dispute and he and his wife were now wandering the world.

"When I left my city," he screamed hoarsely, "the gods gave me a message. 'Go south,' they said. 'Cross the mountains. Find a ruler and offer him your services.'" He hesitated. He had thought about this last night but he still hadn't mentioned it to Joanne. "I think I can be of service to the High Warrior of Imeten. I can fight on the ground as well as your men fight in the trees. I can help you attack your enemies from a new direction."

Jemil Min studied him silently. Reclining on the log, he looked like a serpent with ears. From what Harold had learned of the city's politics, he had to be a shrewd, ruthless man. He had been High Warrior, Nimenlej said, longer than any man in history—ten of the planet's years. In a society in which the rule of every High Warrior had been terminated by rebellion or thinly-disguised murder, that was a spectacular achievement.

"Your knife is made of very fine metal," Jermil Min screamed. "How do you have such a good knife and such a crude mace?"

"I had to leave my city in a hurry. I made the mace with what I happened to have with me."

"Why did you run from the Warrior we sent to welcome you?"

"I didn't know what the gods wanted." He shrugged. "The gods have spoken."

"How do I know you won't run away again?"

"A wise man obeys the gods."

"Do your gods speak through battle also?"

"The gods we worship are as fierce as yours."

"Why won't you eat the food we offer you?"

"It would kill us. We can live only on the food we carry with us."

"Even the Itiji can eat our food. Why are you so different?"

He wiped the sweat off his face. Nimenlej had asked the same question. It seemed to be very important to them. He wasn't sure, but from some of the conversations among the workmen Joanne had overheard, he believed the use of special foods might somehow be connected with a fear that he and Joanne were sorcereres.

"A demon of the lake put a curse on the founder of our city," he said. "He decreed we would die if we ate any food. Only the great god of the mountain—Hail Zeus the Thunderer!—saved us. He wouldn't lift the curse but he made special foods for us and gave us plants and animals which had never existed before. If we eat anything else, we die."

The High Warrior glanced at the council. Harold wished he could read his expression. Nimenlej had questioned him closely, and he had been forced to make the story more and more elaborate. He wasn't sure he could repeat everything he had told Nimenlej without contradicting himself.

"Follow me," Jemil Min screamed.

The High Warrior slid off his couch and trotted toward a curtain at the rear of the hall. The two guards backed up after him and took positions in front of the curtain.

Harold followed Nimenlej through the curtain. The room on the other side was barely three paces square. In the light of a smoky oil lamp, a mace in one hand and a fruit in the other, Jemil Min was already reclining on the only couch.

"Has Nimenlej told you what we do to deserters?" Jemil Min asked.

Harold swallowed. "No."

"We hunt them through the woods as if they were Itiji. When we capture them we torture them with cuts and then we blind them and put them to work in the baths. Now and then we let them rest for a day: we hang them in nets in the sun and let the other men listen to them screaming for water."

"We do similar things in my city."

Jemil Min munched on his fruit. "I've been thinking about what you can do ever since Nimenlej brought you here. Don't repeat anything I'm about to tell you. The only weapon most of the insects out there can use is a slave prod. If they find out about this, I'll probably have to kill half of them."

King Lidris of Drovil, the ruler of a large city further up the river, had added three cities to his domain in the last three years. He was now the strongest ruler in the area and Jemil Min was as certain as if the gods had told him in person that the next city he wanted was Imeten itself. No city had ever been as powerful as Drovil. The Warriors, Harold gathered, had raided and plundered other cities, but they had never actually ruled them. Lidris had invented a formidable new weapon: empire. He now had the armies of four cities at his command.

He also had two iron mines—the mine of Drovil and the mine of Ghanis. If he captured Imeten, he would control all the iron known to the Warriors. All the cities as far west of Imeten as any Warrior had ever ventured would be at his mercy.

The Iron Age was apparently only a few generations old. As the survey from orbit had indicated, there was less iron in the crust of the Delta Pavonis II than there had been in the crust of the smaller world the humans had fled. And of course a people who made most of their fires in the trees were less likely to discover ore by building a fire in a rich dirt and discovering pieces of hot metal in the ashes.

"We are the Warriors of Imeten," Jemil Min screamed. "When people in other cities hear our name, they beg the gods for mercy. Even with four armies, Lidris of Drovil won't attack us until he can arm every man in his forces with an iron mace. The mine of Ghanis is a two-day journey from Ghanis itself. You and Nimenlej are going to raid one of the caravans which take the ore from the mine to the city.

"You will leave in the morning. Nimenlej will explain the strategy to you. If you succeed, you will be rewarded as richly as your commander. We will take good care of your wife while you're gone."

## VII

JOANNE WAS APPALLED. "If it weren't for me, you wouldn't have to do this!"

"If it weren't for you," Harold said, "I'd be dead back on the plateau. It's our only hope, Jo. We're in that kind of a world. To these people you're either a warrior or a slave."

He didn't tell her the party was going to capture slaves, the Itiji who would be hauling the iron to Ghanis. He didn't tell her he would be under the same autocratic discipline as Nimenlej's other subordinates.

When the raiding party assembled by their hut in the morning, Nimenlej had a surprise for him: two large, wheeled wagons. "We'll transfer the ore to them," Nimenlej said. "The Ghanisans will expect us to move much slower and they'll send men out from the city to stop us. They'll think we've been carried away by the gods."

Harold nodded. The wagons were crude but they would probably move at least twice as fast as a loaded sled. He squatted beside the front one and examined the wheel and the axle construction.

He looked up. The lead Itiji in the four slave team was staring at him. He glanced back and the orange eyes slid away.

Nimenlej grabbed a rope and started up. "Prepare to march! Assume your places!"

The men lounging in the trees rose to all fours. The two slavemasters slid down vines and climbed into the wagons.

Joanne started to climb down the ladder in front of their treehouse.

"Forward!" Nimenlej screamed. "Follow me!"

The slavemasters drove their prods into their teams. The wagons rolled forward. Joanne stopped on the ladder and looked down.

Harold backed away behind the second wagon. "Take care of yourself," he yelled in their own language. "I'll be back. I love you."

He couldn't see her face. She had planned to come down and kiss him goodbye as soon as he finished discussing the march with Nimenlej.

She waved slowly. "Be careful. I love you."

He walked backward until the trees finally came between them. Loneliness closed in on him like night closing in on the forest.

Discipline on the march was just as harsh as the discipline he had observed ever since he and Joanne had been captured. The threats and commands Nimenlej screamed at his men stabbed at his emotions like a spur. Every time a prod dug into an Itiji's side, his hands drifted toward the mace and the short sword Nimenlej had given him. The more he watched the tree-dwellers behave, the more he wanted to get out of this situation.

His overactive brain had produced a theory about tree-dweller psychology which added to his anxiety. On Earth, bi-pedal walking had narrowed the human pelvis, and some theorists had felt that one change in anatomy had been a major reason human children were more helpless at birth than the young of any other terrestial animal. The human child was not born with a fully developed brain; the head of the newborn child could pass through the narrow opening in the mother's pelvis only because a major portion of the brain grew after birth.

The tree-dweller women he had seen had broad pelvises. Their children could probably scamper around and create havoc almost from birth. Under primitive conditions, the children who had survived probably had had parents who were good disciplinarians, instead of parents who felt tender, protective emotions toward helpless infants. Affection had had little survival value; reward and punishment had been the only social techniques the circumstances had demanded.

It was a chilling theory. Before they left Imeten he wanted to test it by observing the behavior of very young Imeten children. It would have helped if he had known more about the psychology which had developed on Earth between 1990 and 2022, but unfortunately that had all been forbidden knowledge.

The nights were worse than he had expected. He couldn't sleep alone anymore. All the anxieties which had been dulled during the day by the rhythm of the march assailed him as soon as he stretched out in his sleeping bag. He knew what they would do to punish him if he stepped out of line. They had her at their mercy.

On the third evening of the march—just before the rough-house usually began—he sauntered across the campsite and stood under the branch on which Nimenlej was reclining.

"My Lord."

Nimenlej hung his head over the side of the branch. Harold had deliberately picked the time when he was just getting comfortable for the evening. He usually lay on his branch and watched the games in silence.

"What is it?"

"I've been thinking. If I'm going to drive the Ghanisan slaves when we make the raid, I should do some practice slave driving before we get there."

THE TREE LORD OF IMETEN

"It's almost dark. Why didn't you think about this earlier?"

"If I did it during the day, I might slow down the march. A few minutes every night should be enough. I've been watching the slavemaster while I walked."

Nimenlej moved restlessly. "Get a slavemaster. Tell him I said to rouse one of the teams."

The slavemaster for the first team was lying on a branch above the wagons. He climbed down a rope, grumbling all the time, and prodded his team awake.

"Get up. We're going for a stroll."

The Itiji slept tied to the two poles which connected them to the cart. Crossbraces which kept them from gnawing each other's bonds held the two poles apart. Even if they had managed to gnaw the rope which bound the poles to the tree, they would probably have starved to death in the forest.

The leader of the team stood up silently. The others made soft noises in their own language. All Itiji still looked alike to Harold, but he had the feeling he would have recognized the leader anywhere. In addition to several distinctive scars on his side, he was bigger than the others and he seemed to carry himself with more dignity. He didn't vent his every emotion through his mouth, as the others did. Harold had noticed Nimenlej sometimes bypassed the slavemaster and gave him orders directly.

The slavemaster hooked the poles to the cart. He climbed in and held himself semi-erect on a special bar attached to the front and Harold jumped in beside him. The Itiji stood at the ready position: eyes forward, legs straight, backs perfectly horizontal.

The slavemaster handed him the prod. "Use it every time you give an order. If you want them to turn left, prod the leader on the left. If you want them to go faster, prod him hard in the head. Don't spoil them."

Harold prodded the lead Itiji. "Go!" He had to force himself to do it. The prod disgusted him.

"Harder!" the slavemaster screamed. "Don't be so clumsy. You've got hands. Use them like you've got a stomach."

To the Imetens the stomach was the seat of intelligence. Harold started to snap back and then relaxed. He smiled to himself and gave the Itiji another clumsy prod.

They drifted away from the camp. Every mistake Harold made took them further into the forest. Soon the campfires were a long way back. The first thin mist of the night closed in on the wagon.

The slavemaster continued his invective. He kept jerking the prod out of Harold's hand to show him what to do with it. His language got stronger as Harold kept quiet, and his confidence grew.

"Turn back. We're too far from the camp."

Harold glanced back. The campfires were lost in the mist and the darkness. He leaned forward and prodded the lead Itiji. "Go left."

The prod slid along the smooth flank and rammed the round head at the base of the skull. The Itiji jumped. He looked back at the wagon and his mouth opened silently.

The slavemaster jerked the prod out of Harold's hand. "Insect! Clumsy, crippled groundlife!"

Harold turned on him with a snarl. "Mind your place, inferior! Do you you want your tongue cut out?"

The slavemaster quivered. The end of the prod swung toward Harold's face.

It could have been an involuntary gesture. Harold didn't wait to find out. He jerked the prod out of the slavemaster's hand and hit him in the face as hard as he could.

The slavemaster's eyes closed. His hand slid off the bar. Harold grinned happily and hit him again.

The slavemaster tumbled over the side of the wagon. After a moment he looked up and rose groggily to all fours. His hand moved toward the spear on his back.

Harold drew his sword. "You can walk back. You're lucky. Act like this again and I'll have you pulling the cart yourself."

The slavemaster reached for his spear. Harold leaned over the side of the wagon and slashed. The heavy iron blade chopped through the wooden shaft. The slavemaster threw himself to one side to avoid a cut.

Harold poked the lead Itiji in the rear. "Go!"

The Itiji had all been watching but they turned their heads as soon as his voice snapped. The cart rumbled forward. He looked back and saw the slavemaster scrambling up a tree.

He called a halt as soon as he thought they were temporarily safe. He jumped out of the wagon and walked to the front of the team with his sword in one hand and his mace in the other.

"Do you want to be free?"

Four pair of orange eyes stared at him. He waited but they didn't answer. The two in the rear shuffled restlessly.

He searched for words in Imeten. His heart pounded. For all he knew they liked being slaves. On Earth after one or two generations slaves had often had all their drive for freedom eradicated by their upbringing.

"They have my wife in their power. I can't escape with her—she's crippled and she holds me up. If you could help me by pulling her cart, I could do things for you. I can cut your ropes for you. I can help you fight the Imetens and I can pole you across the river on a raft."

One of the Itiji in the rear said something in their language.

Teeth flashed in the darkness. The leader turned his head and spoke several words.

Harold glanced at the trees. His eyes strained for some sign that Nimenlej was coming.

"We don't have much time," he said. "They'll be here any minute. Do you want to be free?"

"Does a tree want to grow?" the leader screamed in Imeten. "Does a bird want to fly?"

"Then you'll help me?"

"The others are afraid we can't trust you."

"I need you. I can't get away without you."

"How do we know you won't keep us tied to this thing? Don't your people have slaves?"

"I hate slavery. My people left their first city to escape it. Even the gods we worship hate it."

The leader turned to the others. For a moment all four of them seemed to be talking at once. Heads bobbed up and down. Paws scraped the ground.

The leader turned back to Harold. "We believe you." He paused. "I've met you before. You gave me the scars on my side."

Harold blinked. "If it hadn't been for my wife, I would have gone on fighting. She saved both your life and mine. We owe her something."

"Do you want to escape now?"

Temptation tugged at his heart. "No. There'll be another raid. I want time to plan and make sure I've thought of everything. We'll only get one chance. They won't think about us cooperating until they actually see it."

"Nimenlej is tired. With four of us pulling you, we could get back to Imeten hours ahead of them."

"We can't afford a mistake. Nimenlej acts like he trusts you. Do you think he'll take you on other raids?"

"Definitely. He doesn't hate us as much as he pretends."

"We'll wait until the next raid. Let's go back to camp."

"Are you sure there'll be another raid?"

"If this one succeeds there will be. If it doesn't, we'll try an escape on the way back."

He jumped into the wagon. Torches were flickering in the trees. "Head toward the torches," he said. "If I can't talk to Nimenlej—be ready to run."

The cart rolled toward the lights. A voice shrieked the alarm. Other voices picked it up and the torches converged on them.

"What's going on here?" Nimenlej screamed.

Harold guided the Itiji to Nimenlej's branch with the prod. "Your slavemaster was insubordinate," he screamed back. "In my city he would have been killed for that."

Hs eyes peered upward through the mist. The torches had him encircled.

"Slavemaster!" Nimenlej screamed. "Here!"

The slavemaster scurried through the leaves and slapped the branch before his superior. "My Lord! The two legs—"

"Silence! Do you want your tongue cut out? Insect! Groundlife!"

Angry words scorched the slavemaster's crouching back. "Go back to camp, Harold!" Nimenlej ordered. "The next time you have any complaints, tell me! I'm in charge of discipline in this group."

Harold didn't answer. He prodded the Itiji and the cart rolled forward. He had observed the tree-dwellers e-nough to know incidents like this happened all the time. No one would think it was important. He had even been abused less than seemed to be customary; his status with Jemil Min must be high enough to make Nimenlej cautious.

## VIII

THEY APPROACHED THE enemy road in the night. They halted a couple of kilometers from the place where the caravans usually camped for the night and scouts went ahead to spy.

There were three sleds at the camping place. The scouts said they looked like they were heavily burdened. There seemed to be more guards than usual—at least four times eight, one scout said.

"There will be two of them for every one of us," Nimenlej told his men. "Normally we couldn't break through their lines. This time, however, we have Harold. Forget about the ore. Concentrate on killing Ghanisans. You can even retreat a little and draw them away from their sleds. Use your stomachs and fight hard and we'll win. We'll come back heroes from a raid the High Warrior himself ordered."

They left the carts and the Itiji with the slavemaster and moved forward. Nimenlej stalked along the lower branches just above Harold's head. Far above both of them the infiltrators slipped through the upper branches of the trees.

The enemy campfires glowed in the mist. A rope brushed against his face—Nimenlej's signal to halt—and he stopped and knelt behind a tree. He was still about two hundred meters from the camp. The fires in the trees were all he could see of it.

He looked up at the dark canopy above his head. For a moment the gods of battle were as real to him as they were to any of the Imetens poised in the trees. He blew Joanne a kiss and raised his mace at the invisible sky.

The rope brushed his face again. Nimenlej had returned from a last-minute inspection of his men. The dartblowers should be puffing their first darts at the enemy sentries.

A startled voice shrieked the alarm. "Attack!" Nimenlej screamed. "For the Goddess and the City! Conquer and kill!"

Rattles and horns clamored. The Ghanisans sprang to arms. The Imetens swung down from the upper branches screaming battle cries. A horde of panic-stricken small life stampeded through the leaves.

The rope brushed his face. He stood up and moved forward. Ahead of him smoke bombs made from the leaves of certain plants were falling on the camp.

He stepped behind a tree and located the enemy sleds. The rope danced in front of his eyes. "Go!" Nimenlej screamed.

He plunged into the smoke with his sword in one hand and his mace in the other. Bellowing like an animal, he leaped onto a sled.

Two Ghanisans were crouching on the sled on three legs with their weapons drawn. They screamed and a third guard appeared on top of the ore. Harold twisted away from a spear thrust and shoved another spear aside with his sword. His mace caved in a skull. A long arm pushed a sword toward his stomach. He caught it on his own blade, iron grinding on iron, and stepped toward the upturned face grimacing at him through the smoke. His sword plunged into the Ghanisan's shoulder. A wild, gurgling shriek tore at his nerves. He jerked the blade out and turned. The third guard pulled back his spear and fled.

He picked up the prod stuck in the ore pile and poked at the ribs of the Itiji. His voice roared orders in the language of Ghanis. "Go! Go!" The Itiji pushed against their bonds and the huge pile of ore edged forward. He felt as if the prod were jabbing into his own ribs.

He goaded them toward the place where he had left Nimenlej. A rope dropped on him from a tree. He raised his sword and an Imeten slavemaster descended hand over hand through the smoke.

The slavemaster jumped onto the sled. Harold handed over the prod and he shoved it into the flanks of the Itiji. They howled with pain and the sled heaved forward.

A spear flew past his face as he ran toward the second sled. He jumped aboard with both weapons flailing. He slashed through a spear arm and crushed a shoulder and the guards fell back. Holding them at bay with his sword, he picked up the prod and jabbed at the Itiji.

"Go! Go!"

Danger made him jab as hard as any slavemaster. The Itiji howled and threw themselves against their bonds. Prodding with one hand and fighting with the other, he tried to guide them toward Nimenlej.

They wouldn't veer left. He jabbed them as hard as he could on their left flanks but they kept moving straight ahead. They had seen their chance. They were trying to escape.

Ghanisans dropped on the sled. Swords and spears stabbed at his flesh from three sides. The two guards who had been following the sled leaped at his back.

He jumped off the sled. They hopped off after him and closed in. He swung at a sword arm with his mace. His blade slid along a wrist and he twisted away from three searching spear points.

A voice screamed an Imeten battle cry in his ear. Nimenlej charged in, swinging his mace. They fought toward the sled side by side and the Ghanisans fell back before them.

They backed onto the sled. Harold held off the Ghanisans and Nimenlej hooked his mace in his belt and grabbed the prod.

"Move left!" Nimenlej screamed at the Itiji. "Left or I'll blind you."

The prod poked at an Itiji's eye. The Itiji howled and the team veered to the left.

A pair of Ghanisans swung at them on ropes. Harold crouched and met the attack with both weapons. Bodies curled around the ropes; they swung toward him with their maces held in front of them and their feet poised to kick. He sidestepped and stabbed at one of them as the screaming body hurtled by. A foot glanced off his head. He whirled on the other one and swung blindly with his mace. Iron glanced off bone. He opened his eyes and chopped a spear thrust at him by a spearman who had run at the sled while he was off-guard.

They inched out of the smoke, fighting all the way. Again one of the slavemasters climbed down a rope and took charge of the sled.

Hard, heavy fruits dropped on him from the trees as he ran toward the last sled. Voices screamed orders in the language of Ghanis. Spearmen slid out of the branches on ropes and formed a bristling line in front of the sled.

"Turn back!" Nimenlej screamed at him. "Enough! Come back!"

The spearmen charged. He turned around and fled through the smoke. The screams of the slavemaster guided him toward the sleds.

He fell in behind the last sled and walked backward with his weapons ready. Nimenlej was in the trees giving orders. The Imetens were the defenders now. Judging by the screams and the bodies falling from the trees, most of the fighting was now in the lower branches and a few meters behind the sleds. The sleds seemed to be inching away from it.

"Watch your right!" the slavemaster screamed.

He jerked his head around. Dark, low shapes were trotting at the sled from the side.

He stepped in front of them and met them with sword and mace swinging. Spears pressed on him from all sides. He beat his way through them and stayed on the move. They had longer arms and the points of their spears seemed to thrust at him every way he turned, but on the ground in the open he could evade their three-legged shamble with ease as long as he kept backing away from the sled. They didn't want to attack his two arms any more than he wanted to attack four of theirs.

He glanced at the sled. Two Ghanisans armed with swords were crouching on the ore. The slavemaster had dropped his prod and was trying to fight them off with his spear.

A sword splintered the slavemaster's spear. He jumped off the sled and ran toward a tree. Harold roared. His tired arms flailed. The spearmen poked at him defensively and shuffled backward. He struggled toward the sled like a bound man straining against his ropes.

The two swordmen on the sled peered at him through the darkness. One was already prodding the Itiji. The other screamed a challenge and hopped onto the ground to help the spearmen.

Nimenlej swung out of the trees onto the ore. His mace crashed into the Ghanisan with the prod. The Ghanisan who had jumped off the sled heard the grunt of pain and shuffled around. Nimenlej dropped his mace and his hand whipped toward his spear. The Ghanisan on the ground shrieked as the shaft plunged into his shoulder.

Harold whirled on the spears closing in behind him. Step by step he backed toward the sled.

## IX

THE SLEDS CREPT away from the battle in the trees. Harold walked backward behind them and fought off the half-hearted attacks of the spearmen. Eventually the spearmen dropped back and the battle in the trees was lost in the darkness.

He helped the slavemasters load the ore into the wheeled wagons. It was a backbreaking job and it took longer than he had expected. The short-handled Imeten shovels were awkward tools for him and the Imetens themselves couldn't work much faster. He cursed as much as they screamed. His only consolation was the way the slavemasters complained about doing slave work.

A messenger came back from the battle line and watched from the trees as they worked. As they loaded the last wagon and hitched up the captured Itiji, he raced back to Nimenlej with the news.

By morning they were well ahead of their pursuers. A few of the guards were still trailing them but the rest had gone back to Ghanis to fetch reinforcements. Aside from one brief skirmish on the second day—probably some Ghanisan officer's desperate attempt to regain status—they returned to Imeten with no more violence.

The High Warrior gave them all gifts. Everyone in the city had to attend a ceremony in their honor in the main grid. "The gods have spoken!" the High Warrior screamed. "The iron of Ghanis belongs to us. The gods want us to have it. Obey the gods!"

Joanne greeted him with tears. She didn't say it, but she had probably been trembling all the time he was gone. He told her about his conversation with the Itiji as soon as he could.

He lay beside her on the floor of the hut and thought about the risks he had taken. He couldn't do it again. If he had died, she would have been left alone in a strange, savage environment—and a prisoner at that. He saw her living here blinded, and his face twisted in agony.

She rolled over and looked down at him. "What's the matter?"

"Nothing. It's all right. Just a delayed reaction."

She squeezed his hand. "We'd better leave here soon."

"We will. The next time I go on a raid, be ready to leave the second I come back."

He spent the next few days thinking about alternate escape routes and the tactics he would have to use. He did everything he could to improve his acquaintance with Nimenlej. He wanted the Eight Leader to think of him as a fellow Warrior, a being who thought and acted like a tree-dweller.

He listened patiently as Nimenlej complained about the discussions taking place in the Council. The Great Priest and many of the senior Warriors were whispering that the iron raids would be the ruin of Imeten. The gods had spoken, but the Great Priest apparently felt their message had been misinterpeted. The High Warrior was giving Lidris of Drovil an excuse to attack the city, the Great Priest was warning. With an enemy like Lidris, they should be more cautious. Sometimes the gods set traps to tempt the reckless.

As Harold had gathered, there were two ruling classes in Imeten. High Warriors and Great Priests had been feuding as long as both offices had existed. Religion and warfare were so entangled that the lines of authority had never been completely separated.

Despite the enmity of the two classes, there were always ambitious Warriors who hoped to overthrow the current High Warrior with the aid of the priests. Jemil Min's predecessor had been a "priest's mace" and the Great Priest had never forgiven Jemil Min for ending a long period of priestly dominance.

The High Warrior was engaged in a never-ending struggle to hold his position. One slip and Jemil Min would meet the fate of his predecessor, whom he had personally speared after a year of plotting. The Warriors might be far-sighted enough to know they had to weaken Lidris, but many of them were siding with the ambitious senior Warriors who were being supported by the Great Priest. A new High Warrior would mean new status for everyone.

Five days after they had returned to Imeten, Harold said goodbye to Joanne once again.

When he climbed down from the hut the scarred Itiji was leading the first team. They exchanged a swift, meaningful glance as he took his place next to the first wagon. He looked back at Joanne and gave her the thumbs-up sign.

As he ate breakfast on the morning of the third day, he casually watched the slavemasters hitching the Itiji to the wagons. Above him Nimenlej and his assistants were screaming orders. All the Imetens except the slavemasters were in the trees. It was the moment of maximum confusion; the men had finished breakfast but they hadn't fallen into line yet.

He strolled to the front of the scarred Itiji's team. He leaned over the poles as if he were examining something.

"Are you ready?"

"Now?" the Itiji mumbled.

"When I say go."

He stood up. The slavemaster was staring at him.

"I thought he had an insect on his neck."

"He'll tell us. Leave him alone."

He walked back to the wagon. The two Itiji in the rear glanced from him to the Imetens in the trees. Their lips curled.

He jerked his mace off his belt as he stepped onto the wagon. "Go!"

The Itiji howled. The wagon lurched forward. The slavemaster tried to dodge and the mace landed on his back. He shrieked with pain and Harold swung again at the back of his head.

The Itiji had swung the wagon around. They galloped past the second wagon as he pushed the dead slavemaster overboard. The other slavemaster stared at them dumfoundedly.

"Follow us!" the scarred Itiji yelled.

The leader of the second team turned his head after them. His team-mates howled and pushed against their bonds. The slavemaster stunned the leader with a savage thrust of his prod, hopped out of the wagon and held a spear against his throat. Four pairs of longing eyes watched the runaways rumble toward Imeten.

"Stop them!" Nimenlej screamed. "Treason! Desertion! *Dartblowers! Spearmen!*"

A dart flew past the side of the wagon. Harold dropped to his hands and knees. The Itiji yelled something in their own tongue.

He pulled out his sword. The wagon was loaded with provisions and extra weapons and there were several hides to protect the equipment from the rain. He cut the ropes around the biggest hide without getting up and tugged it off the food it was protecting. It was a good tough material.

Darts flashed through the air like silver insects. He stood

up and threw the hide as if he were shaking out a blanket. It dropped heavily on the rear Itiji. They howled with surprise and the leader looked back at him.

"It's to protect you from darts!"

He dropped to his hands and knees again. His sword slid across the ropes which bound another hide. His hands were steady but his heart was hammering. One paralyzing dart in an Itiji's flesh and it would all be over.

He stood up and heaved the hide over the front Itiji. Darts hung harmlessly in the loose folds of the first hide. Even under the covering he could still see the rhythmic rise and fall of the powerful Itiji shoulders.

Two more darts flickered past and landed in the hides. The cart bounced over a root and the hide over the rear team started slipping off.

He squinted at the trees. He couldn't see any Imetens but he could hear them crashing through the branches. Nimenlej was screaming orders and birds and animals were squawking as they hurried out of the way. The second cart was already lost in the trees.

He stepped over the front of the wagon and crouched on the left pole. Holding on with one hand, he tugged the hide back into place.

"Are you all right?" he yelled.

"Is that you on the pole?" the leader asked. His hindquarters were showing but his head was completely covered.

"Yes. Is it too much weight?"

"It's slowing us down some."

"I had to straighten the hides. Can you see?"

"Yes. Are they close?"

"We're out of spear range. We'll be out of dart range soon."

"Did the other team come?"

"No."

He listened for the Imetens above the rumble of the wagon wheels and the rattle of the equipment he had loosened. The ground slid past the tossing hides. Even with the heavily-loaded wagon they were well ahead of their pursuers.

He climbed into the wagon and huddled against a hide. Minutes passed. He stared at the trees slipping past and made himself relax. Above him the morning sun filtered through the leaves. The screams of the Imetens faded.

He stood up and started throwing gear overboard. "How much food will you need?" he asked the leader.

The Itiji exchanged comments in their own language. The hide slid off the leader's head as he looked back. "We'll get our own. We've had enough of their food."

"Will you have time to hunt? We've got to get to Imeten hours before they do."

"We can go without food until tomorrow if we have to. We will not eat slave food again!"

He kept the waterbags and a few extra spears and maces, and the slavemaster's quiver and dartblower. The Itiji didn't speed up as the load grew lighter, but on the other hand they hadn't slowed down since they sprinted out of the camp. If they could keep up this pace, Nimenlej would be hours behind by nightfall.

The leader looked back. "There's the other wagon!"

Harold crouched behind the back of the wagon and peered through the trees. He could just make it out in the pattern of light and shade. It was about two or three hundred meters back.

"How many are in it?"

"Can't you see?"

"No."

"It's Nimenlej and two others."

"Will the other team help us if we stop and fight?"

"No."

"Why not?"

"They have his wife."

Nimenlaj had probably lightened the second wagon as soon as he realized the Imetens couldn't catch them on foot. He looked as though he were driving his team at top speed. If he slowed down now and stayed behind them, they would spend the next three days racing toward their execution. If he left them and went directly to Imeten and the High Warrior, he might even get there first.

"Slow down," Harold yelled. "Keep them behind us. We can't lose them."

He crawled to the front of the wagon and took the dart-blower and quiver off their hooks. He would have traded every weapon on the wagon for his bow and two arrows.

The leader looked back. "You're going to fight them?"

"I'll try to paralyze one of their team. These things don't kill, do they?"

"They hurt. I've been hit by them twice."

"I can't do anything else. If we don't stop them, we might as well forget about my wife."

"Do what you have to do."

"Let them come as close as the distance between two trees."

He crawled to the rear of the wagon. The leader gave an order and the team slowed down. He puffed through the dartblower a couple of times and put his hand in front of the tube to see whether he was generating much thrust.

He watched Nimenlej creep closer. Dart range seemed to be about a hundred meters. The distance he had given the Itiji would be about seventy.

He picked up a scrap of hide he had saved and wrapped it around his head. They were close enough now so he could see that Nimenlej was prodding the team himself. He had apparently brought two dartblowers with him.

Nimenlej screamed an order. His wagon veered to the left. One of the dartblowers raised his weapon. They were just far enough to one side so that he might be able to land a dart on Harold's team.

Harold scurried forward to make sure the hides were in place. He let out a yell. One of the rear Itiji had turned his head to look at their pursuers and the hide had slipped enough to expose his outside flank from the shoulders forward.

The leader looked back at him. The Itiji who had exposed himself went on watching the Imetens.

He pointed at the hide. He couldn't keep his anger out of his voice. "Veer to the left. Get the wagon between you and them. Stop and let me get this fixed."

The leader glanced at the exposed Itiji. They turned sharply. The leader picked up the pace and they galloped around a big tree and stopped short.

Harold jumped out. The tree trunk would protect him until Nimenlej was almost abreast.

He jerked the hide over the Itiji's head. "Don't let him do that again! Doesn't he know what we're doing?"

The leader turned on the offender and roared. His claws scraped the ground as if he wanted to rip the planet to pieces.

Harold jumped back on the wagon. The leader howled and they lurched forward and picked up speed.

He crawled to the back of the wagon and picked up the dartblower. Nimenlej was about fifty or sixty meters away. He was jabbing his prod into his Itiji as if he were punishing them for disobedience.

He stuck a dart in the rear end of the blower and tried

to aim over the back of the wagon. The front end of the tube moved up and down with every bounce.

"Turn back!" Nimenlej screamed. "I won't tell the High Warriors! I swear it! We'll go on together and finish our mission!"

Both the dartblowers in the other wagon had their weapons at their lips. He filled his cheeks with air and blew. Two darts flashed toward him.

He dropped behind the backboard. "Are the hides all right?" he screamed.

"They're all in place," the Itiji leader yelled.

He raised his head. The other team was still galloping. He blew another dart and ducked.

"Turn back!" Nimenlej repeated. "Remember the punishment for desertion!"

He blew four more darts at them. Every time he raised his head the dartblowers were waiting for him.

He flattened himself on the floor of the wagon and collected the spears and maces he had saved in two clattering piles. "Let them come closer," he screamed at the Itiji. Bring them into spear range. Keep the wagon between you and them. They'll be using spears, too."

"You're going to use spears!" the leader shrieked.

"Yes."

"Who are you going to aim at?"

"Nimenlej. If I aim at the Itiji, it'll be the last thing I do."

The leader roared at the team. They slowed down and Harold crawled to the back of the wagon.

He stood up. For a moment he and the three Imetens stared at each other. He raised the spear above his head and hurled it at Nimenlej.

The dartblowers ducked. Nimenlej jabbed his team with

the prod and they swerved sharply. The spear *thunked* into the side of the wagon and a dartblower popped up.

Harold dropped. He looked up and saw the dart flash over his head. They were too close to miss.

He picked up another spear and looked over the back-board. Both dartblowers had their weapons on him.

"Surrender!" Nimenlej screamed. "I'll have you blinded if you don't surrender!"

He grabbed a half-empty waterbag and pulled it toward him. It was big enough to cover most of his chest. By squeezing the hide together he could get a good grip on the middle.

He stood up with the hide in his left hand. The Imetens screamed. Two darts sped toward him and he hurled the spear.

The darts tapped hollowly on the water bag. An Imeten shrieked as he dropped to the floor. He peeked over the backboard and saw one of the dartblowers falling backwards with a spear in his chest.

Nimenlej thrust the prod at the other dartblower and pulled his spear out of its sheath. He screamed a prayer at the gods. Harold stood up without his improvised shield and they both let fly.

Harold dropped. Nimenlej's spear crashed into the floor of the wagon and quivered in the wood next to his foot. He stared at it as though it had some kind of hypnotic power. When he looked over the backboard, Nimenlej already had another spear in his hand.

Nimenlej screamed an order. The dartblower prodded the slaves and his wagon veered sharply to the left. The right wheel came off the ground. Nimenlej leaned forward and hurled his spear.

"Turn right!" Harold screamed at the Itiji. "He's throwing his spear at you."

The Itiji leader roared. The weapons on the floor of the wagon bounced and clattered as the Itiji swerved.

An Itiji howled. The wagon lurched to a halt. "Tavid's speared!" the leader yelled.

Nimenlej stopped his wagon just out of spear throw. "You can't escape, Harold. Surrender and you won't be blinded. I won't tell the High Warrior."

Harold stood up with the waterbag in front of his chest. Behind him the wounded Itiji was beginning to moan. Nimenlej was brandishing another spear and the Itiji leader was looking at him over the writhing hides and wailing a wild, strange song in his own language.

He jumped out of the wagon and ran back to the team. Nimenlej screamed at him. A dart sailed over his head.

He jerked the hides off the backs of the Itiji. His sword slashed at their bonds. "Fight!" *Thwack!* "Fight for your lives!" *Thwack! Thwack!*

The Itiji burst out of the poles like three howling demons. He held the waterbag in front of his chest and they charged across the dark ground at Nimenlej's spear and the dartblower's tube.

They fanned out and came in from four directions. Nimenlej screamed at them to halt. The Itiji in Nimenlej's team howled. Harold roared. The Itiji running beside him yelled a battle cry which woud have chilled the blood of a Viking.

Darts tapped on the waterbag. Nimenlej heaved his spear. The Itiji on Harold's right rolled over and clawed the ground with a shaft dancing in his side.

Nimenlej drew his sword. The dartblower swung the cattle prod as the Itiji leaped at the wagon. Harold stepped onto the poles binding the slaves and stabbed at Nimenlej.

Nimenlej parried and stabbed back. Iron gnashed on iron.

Behind Nimenlej's back the dartblower went down before the Itiji.

"Deserter! Traitor!"

Nimenlej stabbed. Something hot burned Harold's side and he gasped. He stepped off the pole and dropped to one knee with his sword raised to ward off another blow. A black shape reared up behind Nimenlej's shoulders and knocked the Eight Leader's sword out of his hand.

The dartblower was lying dead and mangled on the ground. The Itiji who had been hit with the spear had stopped moaning. Above him Nimenlej was pinned to the wagon with his arm hanging over the front and the Itiji leader resting heavily on his back.

He clutched his side. Warm blood oozed into his hand.

"Are you all right?" the Itiji leader asked.

He looked at the wound. It was a long slash and there was plenty of blood, but apparently his abdominal wall was still intact. If he could avoid chemical poisoning or a freak infection, it should be healed enough to give him no trouble by the time they reached Imeten.

"It isn't deep. It's bloody but it isn't serious." He stood up and looked at Nimenlej. "Will you surrender or do I have to let him hold you like that until we leave?"

Nimenlej wiggled angrily. Harold tried to find some way to say he was sorry he had to do this but gave up when he realized the only words for regret in the Imeten language implied self-abasement. He shrugged and turned to the Itiji in Nimenlej's team.

"We need two more men to go with us. We'll take all of you if you want to go."

"You'll all be blinded," Nimenlej screamed. "We'll hunt you to the end of the river."

The leader of the team stared down the forest lanes. The other three looked up at the scarred Itiji and said a few words in their own tongue. They understood Imeten but, as slaves, only a few of them were expected to speak it fluently.

"They'll all come but the leader," the scarred Itiji said.

He stepped forward and cut their ropes. "I'll have to tie you to our wagon the best way I can. We don't have time to work out something better. As soon as we're able, I'll arrange the ropes so you can leave the wagon at any time. You aren't slaves anymore. We will work together as males-with-the-same-status."

His sword arm seemed to surge with power. He had rarely felt so glad he was alive.

The Itiji who had been speared in the charge was definitely dead. The other Itiji who had been wounded was still lying in front of the wagon, moaning to himself. The wound in the thigh of his right rear leg looked terrible. Harold bent over it, clutching his own wound, and shook his head.

"We have to put you in the wagon," Harold said. "It's going to hurt but we have to get out of here right away. I'll do what I can for you when we start moving."

"I understand," the Itiji said. "You're wounded, too."

He howled from the moment Harold lifted his shoulders. The spear wobbled constantly. Fresh blood gushed out of the wound.

"See what your friends are like," Nimenlej screamed. "Listen to him."

The wounded Itiji put his forepaws over the side of the wagon. Harold released his shoulders and lifted his rear paws. His own wound hurt every time he twisted or bent but he kept his temper under control. The Itiji probably expressed all their emotions with their voices. For all he knew the creature howling in his ears might be as brave and self-controlled as a silent, stoic human. He had kept his claws sheathed when pain might have made him scratch, and every motion of his body was making the job a little easier.

## X

THEY DIDN'T STOP for several hours. To save time, Harold built a small fire inside the wagon, removed the spear and disinfected both wounds with boiled water while they were moving.

The Itiji pulling the wagon cursed the Imetens for several minutes when he told them he thought the spear had cut a nerve and their friend would never walk again. The rest of their conversation restored most of his satisfaction, however. Apparently a crippled Itiji would always be supported and cared for by his social group.

"He's better at loving and poetry anyway," one of the Itiji pulling the cart said in halting Imeten. "When we get home, he can lie around all day and tell the girls pretty stories."

The wounded Itiji made a face. "He'll be free," the scarred Itiji growled. "Cripple or not, he'll be free. Before I'll be a slave again, I'll lose all my legs."

The scarred Itiji was named Gladvig Ligda Liva. As soon as they had finished expressing their feelings about the wound and the Imetens, he introduced himself and the others with elaborate ceremony. It took him almost half an hour to say everything that had to be said, and they managed to get it all in while maintaining the same pace they had kept up since they left the Imeten camp.

They had been taciturn and silent among the Imetens, but now that they were free they never closed their mouths. If they weren't talking, they were singing. He questioned them about their culture and their history, and they answered with so much enthusiasm that a few questions kept them talking until bedtime.

The contrasts between the two types of intelligent beings fascinated him. As the day wore on he forgot about the danger waiting for them in Imeten and revelled in the heady feeling that his awareness and understanding were expanding at a tremendous rate. He was doing exactly what he had dreamed about when he had stood on the edge of the plateau and stared at the forest.

They took time out to forage on the morning of the second day. He untied the ropes which bound them to the poles, and they disappeared into the forest in five different directions. For the first time since they had left Nimenlej screaming in the forest, they were all silent at the same time. Even the wounded Itiji in the wagon limited himself to breathing.

Harold crouched in the cart and wondered if they were going to return. Why should they care about Joanne? From here on he might be more of a hindrance to them then a help.

A deep-throated howl broke the quiet. Sharp yaps answered from the four corners of the compass. Swift, black shapes slipped through the trees. Howling back and forth, they drew their net around their quarry.

His heart jumped when the animal burst into sight. It was galloping toward the wagon through the shadows of the forest with two Itiji howling on its tail. It was about the size of a large deer but it had a single long horn and its legs were thick and muscular. An Itiji howled behind him just before it reached the wagon, and Liva leaped in front of it and swatted at its nose. It stabbed at him with its horn and veered, and another Itiji darted from behind a tree and turned it again.

They brought it to bay in a circle of noisy huntsmen only a spear-throw from the wagon. Harold's fists clenched with excitement. Liva howled and one of the Itiji charged the animal's hindquarters and dodged as it turned in its own length and kicked at his side with its powerful front legs. For all its weight it was agile as a dancer. In a single flow of motion it kicked both hind legs at an Itiji who came in from its rear, thrust with its horn at the Itiji snarling at its face, and spun on the Itiji trying to reach its flanks.

Sharp teeth snapped at a foot. An Itiji leaped at the animal's neck and twisted away from a thrust of the horn. For an instant one side of the tawny neck was exposed. Liva leaped in and slashed at its throat. The animal shrieked. Two heavy bodies crashed into its side and bore it to the ground.

He had trouble watching them eat. They were polite and ceremonious, but they had never invented fire.

They dismembered the part they didn't eat with deft stokes of their claws and he wrapped it in a hide and tied it under the wagon for them. Later in the day they added more tidbits to their diet by stopping to rob a colony of bird nests.

The way they talked about food filled him with envy. He had been living on cheese fungus since he had left the mountains and they insisted on talking about all the meals they had eaten in the past and planned to eat in the future.

They despised the diet the Imetens had fed them. Eating was not the least of the many things freedom meant to them.

"I admired the way you brought that animal down," Harold said. "If the Imetens think you're cowards, either they're blind or they've never watched you hunt."

"They know how brave we are," Liva said. "Why do you think they stay in the trees until they've got us paralyzed or tangled in nets? It's been a long time since any Imeten hunted us on the ground for sport. If we had weapons and they had to face us on the ground, they'd avoid us as if we were the gods themselves."

Harold felt uncomfortable. He was going to return to the mountains and relative safety, but what were the Itiji returning to? Their species was probably doomed. In the grim process of evolution, weapons counted more than graciousness and a strong sense of community.

Or did they? If humans had been a little more like Itiji, they might not have ruined everything they had built on Earth—and his father and Walt Sumi might still be alive.

He changed the subject. "Are all the animals you hunt as dangerous as that one?"

"I would have waited for an easier quarry if we had time. We don't hunt those normally unless we have at least eight hunters. You can't kill them quickly with a small group unless someone risks his life."

They circled Imeten in the night. Twice they had to hide in the shadows while a patrol trotted by above Only the keen senses of the Itiji warned them in time. He might be their hands, but they were his eyes, ears and legs.

He marched up to the treehouse as if he were coming back from the fields for lunch. He had his sword and his mace and he had stuck a few of the slavemaster's paralyzer darts in his belt.

Four guards were squatting in the branches around the house. He waved hello jauntily.

"Where are the others?" the guard leader screamed.

"I left them at the Itiji stockade. We had to come back."

Joanne stuck her head out the door. He smiled up at her and she waved and blew him a kiss. One of the guards rushed off as he climbed the ladder.

She pulled him into the house. He put his hands on her shoulders and held her at arms' length. "We're going. Are you ready?" He wanted to kiss her but he didn't dare. He didn't want to be tempted into lingering the few seconds that might spoil everything.

"I've got everything we need, except the rabbits, in one bag," Joanne said. "What do you want me to do?"

He handed her the mace and several darts. "You can throw the darts by hand at this range. They don't kill; they just paralyze temporarily. When I shout, step out the door and throw one at the nearest guard. The Itiji will run out of the trees as soon as they hear me." He hesitated. "Use the mace if you have to. Don't be squeamish."

She swallowed. "I won't."

"There are three of them. One just left for the city. Get rid of them fast and we'll be gone before anybody else gets here."

He stepped through the door and started climbing the ladder as if he were going to the city. The guard leader crouched on his branch and watched him carefully. One guard was squatting on a thick branch near the door; the third was hidden from him by the leaves of the shadows.

His right hand sneaked toward his belt. He twisted on the ladder and flung a dart at the leader.

"Joanne! Liva!"

The guard leader reached for his spear and tried to shuffle

to one side. Harold reached for another dart. The guard leader stiffened and toppled backward off the branch.

Joanne was leaning out of the house. The guard who had been posted opposite the door was sprawled on his branch. The Itiji were galloping toward the house.

Harold searched for the third guard. "Be careful, Jo."

She ducked into the house. "Can you see him? He's on my left. In that cluster of vines."

"Where the big yellow flower is?"

"Yes."

A face broke through the vines. A spear aimed and ready to throw pointed at him from beside the right ear.

He slid around the rough bark of the tree. "Throw the mace at him," he yelled. "We don't have time to play games."

He held onto the ladder nailed to the tree and watched the front of the house. Joanne leaned out and hurled the mace at the cluster of vines. It crashed through the foliage and the guard scrambled out of the way. For a second sunlight glistened on his head and shoulders.

Harold tossed a dart at him. The spear dropped from his hand. He stiffened and plummeted through the leaves.

Joanne dropped the bundle and the rabbit cages. In the distance, Imeten voices screamed faintly.

They scrambled down the ladder. He jumped into the wagon and pulled Joanne up after him. Liva howled and they rumbled into the trees.

They lurched to a stop less than a hundred meters from the house. The Itiji turned around and looked at them.

"What's the matter?" Harold asked.

Liva glanced toward the city. The screams were getting louder. "We are freeing your wife, Harold. We came back here just for her. My wife is still in the stockade—a slave! I don't want to leave her any more than you wanted to leave your wife. By the laws of gods I shouldn't leave her. Will you come back and help me free her?"

Harold glanced at Joanne. She nodded slowly.

"We'll come back," Harold said. "I swear it."

The Itiji howled. They leaped against their traces and the wagon shot forward. Behind them Imeten voices screamed battle cries.

## XI

*This is the song every child must learn. Sing it with fervor. It is the song of gratitude.*

*They came out of the north walking on two legs. The first time Liva saw them, they frightened him more than all the armies of the tree-dwellers. The strange thing they were pulling said they could make tools and weapons no creature who could speak had ever seen. They could work and fight with both hands at the same time. They were more terrible than the sun, more frightening than death and loneliness. Every living thing was at their mercy.*

*And this was the gift of the gods: that they were brave and could act, and wise and could foresee.*

*This is the song of wonder, the song of Harold and Joanne . . . .*

At the resting place on the road from the iron mine to Imeten, the embers of campfires glowed in the trees. Bone-weary Itiji slaves slept in their bonds beside their overloaded sleds. Imeten guards crouched at their posts or paced restlessly from branch to branch.

# THE TREE LORD OF IMETEN

Two kilometers away, Harold and Joanne moved from Itiji to Itiji, fastening shields of wood and hide on each muscular back. Orange eyes glowed in the darkness. Choked voices murmured their reactions to Liva's whispered oration.

"Some of us will die tonight," Liva was saying. "Some of us will never again enjoy our wives, never again run singing through the forest, never hunt and eat the good food the gods have given us. The words some of us might have spoken will never be heard."

Harold listened as he worked. He would never master the Itiji languages as well as he had mastered Imeten, but he had learned the language Liva was speaking well enough to follow it, and he liked the rhythms and the deep, rich sounds. The fourteen Itiji who were listening were exploding with emotion, but they automatically fitted their responses into the pattern of Liva's oration. As he had learned during many lengthy sessions, the Itiji couldn't move without a speech; if quiet hadn't been absolutely necessary, they would have been singing.

Point by point, as if they had never heard any of it before—and argued it out among themselves every time they had a spare moment—Liva reminded them of the justice of their cause, their right to be free, the long history of their race which every Itiji carried in the phenomenal Itiji memory, and the women and children in every community who would think of them with admiration when the story of their courage became one of the great songs of their people.

"If we fail, someday our species will be silenced forever. The tree-dwellers will do what Harold has prophesied: their weapons will become stronger and stronger, and they will take over all the World and leave us nothing. What does it matter if we live a few years longer and everything our tongues have spoken is eventually forgotten? Treat death with contempt."

Harold rested a shield on an Itiji's back and started buttoning the front straps. Joanne finished the shield she was working on and came over to help.

"This is the last one," she whispered.

He reached across the shield and pressed her hand.

"The gods have sent us Harold and Joanne. Show the gods we are worthy of the gift!"

They buttoned the last strap. Harold picked up his own shield and stepped in front of the line.

"We're ready, Liva."

"Have you heard?" Liva asked. "Do you consent?"

"We have heard," the Itiji murmured. "We consent."

"The sun is rising! Sing the morning prayer!"

Joanne climbed into the wagon. Four Itiji took their places between the poles and the rest spread out in a long skirmish line.

They moved out, with the wagon a few paces in the rear. Harold walked beside Liva with his sword in his right hand and his big oval shield in his left. A light rain brushed across his face, but the ground was still firm; if things went as well as he hoped, they should be far away from the Imetens before the earth got muddy enough to slow down the wagon.

He looked down at the dark shape stalking beside him. Liva had planned for this night since their first conversation; from the moment Harold had asked him if he wanted to be free, he had begun to think about ways the humans could help his species fight the tree-dwellers. With their hands, he had reasoned, they could make weapons which Itiji could use, but which they couldn't make for themselves. He had had a few vague notions about what such weapons might be like, and he had been certain people who were used to working with tools would be able to think of many more.

Their basic strategy had been Harold's idea. He had thought about it before they crossed the river but he hadn't suggested it until they were halfway to the mountains. He and Joanne had discussed it several times before they mentioned it to Liva. If the Itiji accepted the idea, they would be committed to a struggle which might take years.

If they could assemble enough fighters, Harold believed they could harass Imeten so effectively that the Warriors would soon discover they couldn't fight the Itiji and hold back Lidris of Drovil at the same time. To get even a weak force off his back, Jemil Min might be willing to make concessions.

Liva hadn't known enough about the wars of the tree-dwellers to think of such a strategy himself. When Harold had suggested it to him he had roared with excitement. Descriptions of a wonderful future had flowed from his tongue.

Harold had not been happy about the prospect of more fighting. He was proud of the way he had handled himself in combat, but he was no warrior. He had been awed, however, by the importance of the thing. The destiny of an entire species depended on him.

"If we can just force the Imetens to sit down and bargain," Joanne had pointed out, "we'll have accomplished something. We'll have established a new relationship between the Itiji and the tree-dwellers. You don't negotiate with animals."

In the future there would undoubtedly be other exiles from the plateau. If he and Joanne could do something significant for the Itiji, at least one race on this planet would remember humans with gratitude and treat them as friends. And when humans finally left the plateau in large numbers, as they had to sooner or later, a world in which two species lived as equals would accept them much more easily than a world in which one intelligent species dominated another.

Or suppose some of the mechanized savages he had left on the plateau decided they would like to use their superior technology to do a little enslaving themselves? If that day ever came, he wanted the Itiji and the tree-dwellers both to have some evidence that humans could bring a world something better than trouble and suffering.

He had to fight. He had no choice. He was his father's son; he knew a responsibility when he saw one.

*By my troth I care not; a man can die but once; we owe God a death . . . and let it go which way it will, he that dies this year is quit for the next. . . .*

"What are you saying?" Liva muttered. "Is that your language?"

Their hearing amazed him as much as their memory. His lips had hardly been moving.

"It's a verse by one of our poets. It's about death and the gods."

He tried to work out a translation which would do Shakespeare justice. He gave up when he realized the Itiji had no word for *owe* which implied the debt could be paid in full sooner or later. The closest word he could think of— *gliad*—referred to a continuing lifelong obligation to the community.

"I'll translate it later," he whispered. "It's harder than I thought. Different customs make different words."

He dropped back to the cart and walked beside Joanne. She touched his shoulder and the top of his head and he looked up at her face and brushed her hand with his lips.

They had made love just before dawn. At lunch they had baked a rabbit and tasted real meat.

He returned to his place beside Liva. The whispers on either side told him the Itiji could already see the embers of the Imeten fires. Liva sent his orders down the line and black shapes flowed into the night.

He waited by himself in the shadow of a tree. Rain and sweat ran down his face. He glanced back at Joanne and discovered that the wagon was already hidden.

A guard shrieked the alarm. The Itiji howled a hunting song. Swift shadows streaked toward the sleds.

He crouched behind his shield and listened to the song. Each hunter always fitted a terse description of his own actions to the traditional melody. At all times each individual was supposed to know everything that was happening to the group. He had expressed his doubts, but even in warfare the Itiji believed cooperation should be given as freely as possible.

They had surrounded the sleds. The slaves were howling questions at them. Spears and darts were raining on their shields. Teeth were gnawing at the ropes binding the slaves.

The Imetens had been taken by surprise. Confined to the use of one hand hand at a time, they had never invented the shield. They were throwing missiles from the trees as if it were a habit they couldn't break.

An Imeten officer screamed an order. Half the triple eight guarding the sleds slid down ropes and formed a battle line on the ground. The officer screamed a prayer at the gods and they charged the sleds from two sides.

The Itiji formed a circle around the sleds. The snarls and groans of hand-to-hand combat filled the forest. Itiji went down with spears in their bellies and faces clubbed in by the iron weapons of the Imetens. Imetens fell shrieking before mangling claws and teeth.

Every time an Imeten died, Liva roared out the total. Two Itiji were dead but six Imetens had died with them—and more Imetens were lying on the ground, shrieking in pain. The freed slaves were joining in the struggle. Already the hunting song sounded triumphant.

Liva bellowed above the din. The last slave had been freed. Two live, unwounded Imetens were lying on the ground with Itiji standing over them.

Harold ran toward the carnage. He burst out of the night without a sound. Crouched on three legs, the Imetens were thrusting at the Itiji with their weapons and the Itiji were holding them back with swipes of their paws and sudden rushes. Wounded of both races were writhing on the ground.

A voice shrieked his name. He stabbed an Imeten in the back and shoved another out of the way with his shield. Two Itiji stepped apart to let him through the line. A mace slammed the bottom of his shield against his legs and he staggered into the circle.

He bent over the prisoners. The sleds protected him on most of one side and his shield on most of the other; for the rest he would have to depend on the Itiji and the gods.

The two Imetens had been stunned from the back and dragged through the melee by the two Itiji Liva had delagated for the task. They were lying face down in the dirt and each one had an Itiji standing on his shoulders. They had already stopped struggling; they were inferiors, not Warriors, and they had surrendered, after all, the time in their life when it counted most.

He grabbed the ropes which had bound the Itiji slaves and started binding the prisoners' hands and feet. He glanced up and saw Liva brushing a spear aside with his paws. The tree-dwellers were poking at the Itiji lines as if they were going through the motions to appease their officers.

An Itiji howled behind him. He looked back. A slave was writhing on the ground with a spear stuck in his side. *He jumped in front of a spear aimed at Harold,* Liva sang. *Remember his name forever. Gliad! Gliad!*

He laid the edge of his sword on the necks of the two prisoners. The two Itiji jumped off their backs and joined the battle line. "Do what I say," he screamed, "or you'll be killed. Come with us and we'll treat you well. You'll live longer than if you'd stayed in Imeten."

He stood over them with his sword raised and the bottom of his shield resting on the ground. Imetens shrieked curses at him across the line. The Itiji waiting with the wagon burst from their hiding place and galloped out of the rain at the sleds.

The Imetens cried out. The four Itiji pulling the wagon crashed into the battle with their heads pulled back under their shields and their bellies close to the ground. Imetens scrambled out of their way. The poles extended half a meter in front of the front pair and spear points bristled along the crossbar which connected them.

The wagon stopped beside the sleds. The Itiji crowded around it and Harold planted himself in front of the backboard. His shield gave him an overwhelming advantage. The Imetens backed out of his way as through he were brandishing a pistol.

Joanne stepped off the wagon and dragged the prisoners aboard by their shoulders. They shrieked curses at her but they didn't resist. Harold prayed to the gods a freak spear wouldn't slip past his shield and the protecting bulks of the wagon and the ore sleds. He had tried to keep Joanne out of the battle zone but she had insisted that his hands should be used to fight.

An unshielded slave hopped onto the wagon with the prisoners. Joanne started picking up weapons and laying them in the wagon. Above the din Harold heard Liva telling her to pull the spear out of the slave who had saved her husband's life; he would have wanted them to use his death for everything they could use it for.

She climbed into the wagon and crouched on the floor. The Itiji bellowed the music they sang when they dragged the quarry to the ground. The wagon rolled forward and Harold ran beside it and pushed the Imetens back with his sword.

When they counted their dead, they discovered they had left six Itiji lying by the sleds.

## XII

THE ITIJI lived in nomadic communities which wandered the country north of the river. The largest community had about a hundred citizens, and most were smaller, but each community had its own law and political organization, and usually spoke its own language. For thousands of years the Itiji had spent their leisure hours speculating about the universe and experimenting with new social relationships; they lived under every form of government Harold and Joanne had read about, plus several which humans had never invented.

The communities were not isolated, however. They communicated constantly, as their trails crossed and as they met at watering places and hunting grounds, and people often switched from one community to another. The entire country north of the river was actually a single society of fantastic complexity.

Unfortunately no community had emphasized the ideals

of courage and military honor which make men act like warriors. The Itiji had no history of war among themselves, and their linguistic talents had given them such complete mastery of their environment that they had been forced to face few dangers other than disease. Until the coming of the tree-dwellers, they had lived comfortably and easily. Their poems and stories told about sexual relations and family life, exploration, and the beauty of such things as speculative thought and the rhythms and interactions of nature. They had stories in which the hero faced great danger in defense of the community, but they were stories which celebrated social responsibility, not courage.

Only their strong sense of community had made them fight back as hard as they had. They had organized a loose but effective system of passive defense, with communities exchanging information about slaving parties, and scouts watching the river and passing the word when a slaving party crossed, but they had resigned themselves to a steady trickle of losses. The tree-dwellers were a fact of life, like rain and disease. When the will of the gods came armed, it could be discussed, but not defied.

For hundreds of kilometers east and west, Itiji had exchanged rumors about Gladvig Ligda Liva and the two strange creatures with hands, and the small band of young men who had followed Liva and the *humans* across the river. Now Liva led his caravan from community to community and let every Itiji in the land north of Imeten look at the first Imeten prisoners any Itiji had ever captured. His eloquent voice proclaimed the news: The gods had sent allies. The Itiji were unarmed no longer. The days of graceful, gentlemanly acceptance had come to an end.

To Harold and Joanne it was an impressive performance. Liva knew the customs and the language of every community they visited. They sat through endless discussions and ceremonies with Liva's son, Gladvig Liva Dlav, translating for them, and Liva always made his plea at the optimum moment, and used the arguments which would have the maximum impact on the group he was addressing. He knew when to appeal to a community's sense of proportion and grace, and when to remind them that no Itiji ever left another Itiji to die when he could do something to help; and he knew when he should compliment the leader's taste in food or pretty glades, and when he should sing a gay song about sexual pleasure, or flatter the importance of women or the wisdom of democratic groups.

Three or four recruits joined them after every visit. For any attempt to persuade Itiji that was apparently a good record; the hair-splitting and logic-chipping Liva had to listen to drove Harold crazy. If humans had been as hard to lead as Itiji, his father would have been reduced to gibbering rage ten days after the starship left the Moon.

The two prisoners were put to work helping the humans make weapons. Soon four groups of shielded Itiji were patrolling the forest. Harold constructed bows and dartblowers an Itiji could carry on his back while another Itiji loaded and shot with his teeth, and a young genius even designed a shield harness an Itiji could put on and take off without help.

Harold quickly realized that tools were more important then weapons. He and Joanne couldn't possibly arm the forces Liva was raising. With the captured Imeten weapons, he made the Itiji metal knives and saws which could be worked with the mouth. Liva's son designed a hammer, a piece of stone or metal with a glove-like strap into which an Itiji could insert a paw, and the Itiji had everything they needed to make their own shields. Although their only tools had been crude stone knives and such temporary devices as stretchers and sleds made out of bushes, the Itiji seemed to be as mechanically inventive as the Imetens. All they had needed was help with the first developments. They couldn't attach the strap to the hammer, but they could use the gadget when it was given to them—and they could invent it, once they knew there were hands to build it.

They were still on the defensive, but for a few of them at least it had become an active defense. In the past when a slaving party had ambushed an Itiji with a dart or trapped him in a pit or a net, the prisoner's community had been forced to choose between two options—slink away, or make a suicidal attempt to free him and add more victims to the slavers' bag as darts and nets fell on them from the trees. Usually most of the community had slunk away in shame and despair, and the prisoner's immediate family had tried to save him, as had happened when Liva had been taken. Now they could call on one of the groups of shielded fighters instead. The slavers were forced to fight on the ground just to keep their bait.

Casualties were heavy on both sides. For every dead Imeten there was at least one dead Itiji. Two more Imetens were captured, however, and put to work making tools and weapons. And with every successful attack on a slaving party, more Itiji joined the fight.

The humans concentrated on making weapons and tools and supervising the Imeten prisoners. They moved their camp every day. Several double eights had entered the forest and seemed to be looking exclusively for them. Harold kept the camp ready to move at all times. Tools and weapons were put in the wagon as soon as they were completed, and everyone in the party except the captives knew what should be abandoned at once and what should be saved if possible. Every time they made camp he worked out an escape plan with Joanne and the six Itiji who travelled with them.

# THE TREE LORD OF IMETEN

They had one narrow escape. An Imeten patrol almost surrounded them and attacked them by surprise. They would have been wiped out at the start of the struggle if it hadn't been for a lone Itiji who had either been following the patrol or had stumbled on it by accident just before it reached the camp. By the time he got close enough to give the alarm, the Imetens were apparently in position directly above his hiding place. His warning howl ended in a death rattle.

They abandoned the prisoners and the unfinished work and galloped away from the campfire in a hail of missiles. Eventually a passing community discovered the Itiji who had given the warning hanging from a branch with three spears in his body.

They met Liva three days later at one of their periodic conferences. He was as disturbed by the loss of the prisoners as Harold had been. The tools were their biggest problem. It took an Itiji eight days to make a shield, and at the present moment they had only fifty hammer and saw sets.

"If we had enough tools," Liva said, "I could have three hundred men fighting in another eight days. They come to me eager to fight and I have to tell them to wait."

Harold leaned against a tree and rubbed his beard. He glanced at the wagon to make sure Joanne was still taking her nap. He had been doing some arithmetic in his head.

He had always wondered how the generals in the history books could compute human deaths as if they were keeping accounts. Now he thought he understood—it was inherent in the nature of war. Eleven dead Itiji equalled two prisoners. Two prisoners equalled twenty hammers and saws in sixteen days—plus nails, darts, arrows, and the six two-man missile weapons he had built while the prisoners were making the tools. So many tools, so many weapons, equalled so many armed Itiji, equalled so many dead Imetens, equalled victory.

His revulsion was irrelevant. From now on every life but one had a price.

"We need prisoners," he said.

"The last time we captured a prisoner," Liva said, "six men died."

"If we're going to fight, we have to think like fighters. If ten men died to get one prisoner, we've come out ahead. It's a terrible way to think, but if we can't make ourselves do it, all the lives we've already lost will have been lost for nothing."

A guard barked a warning. Harold picked up his shield and Liva rolled over onto his and came up with it resting securely on his back. The guards lying around the camp jumped up.

One of the guards, who had been circling the camp at a distance, was galloping toward them through the trees in the perfect silence Liva had requested—a strenuous discipline for an Itiji.

"Prepare for flight!" Liva howled.

Joanne looked over the back of the wagon. Four Itiji slipped between the poles.

The guard threw himself down on the ground in front of them. His claws tore up the dirt. He threw back his head and wailed his news to the music of a lament as old as the anguish of the Itiji.

"The Imetens have sent an army. Eight times eight double eights crossed the river six days ago. A community is coming toward us escorting a woman. Four double eights surrounded her community and captured them. Two prisoners in every eight were speared. She was beaten and slashed with their swords. Two of the men were blinded."

Harold beat on the ground with the bottom of his shield. Rage blinded him.

Several Itiji were coming toward the camp. Everyone in the area ran out to meet them. The woman who had been tortured limped forward and told her grief to the same music the guard had chosen. Terrible scars covered her face and her sides.

Joanne knelt beside the woman and examined her wounds. "When did it happen?" Liva demanded. "Where are they now?"

"Three days ago," an Itiji said. "They're moving this way. I think her community was the first. We heard about another this morning."

They broke camp and started moving toward the mountains. During the night they encountered a community which was moving in the same direction with three more survivors of an Imeten ambush.

Divided into units of four double eights, the Imeten army scoured the forest. Out of every eight Itiji captured, two were speared and hung from the trees. The minor watering places were fouled and the major ones were guarded. The animals the Itiji hunted were slaughtered wantonly. And after every atrocity the beaten, scarred prisoners were sent into the forest with the same message—bring us the two-legs who gave you the weapons.

In the past the Imetens had come in small bands of slavers and they had killed only when they couldn't avoid it. Now, fielded in the numbers in which they fought battles, with maiming and killing their only objective, they were almost invincible. The five thousand Itiji who lived in the land north of Imeten fled before the storm.

Liva and his handful of fighters did what they could. Against overwhelming odds they stormed into Imeten camps to rescue ambushed communities. Liva's son died trying to pull a paralyzed mother out of a ring of Imeten spearmen. By the time the last community had slipped out of the holocaust, only ten fighting men were left alive.

Harold watched the slaughter put new sorrows in Joanne's eyes. He wondered how he could go on living. He had set out to change the history of a world and instead bodies hung from the trees. Was this the *hubris* of the Greek tragedies, the overweening pride which brought down the wrath of the gods?

Jemil Min's troops cut deep into the lands dominated by Ghanis. The communities which normally roamed the lands north of Ghanis endured some of the punishment intended for their neighbors. Itiji from both territories crowded together in camps. Every minute of the day Harold could hear a funeral song or a child crying for food. On every side cries of despair echoed his own feelings. Outnumbered, outweaponed, short of food, surely they were the sport of the gods!

Liva stalked from camp to camp, calling for men to bear shields and avenge the dead. Was this any worse than what they had endured for generations? Did the people who had been tortured in the raid suffer anymore than the Itiji enslaved in the tree-dweller cities suffered every day?

"Do you see Harold wailing and scratching the dirt?" Liva thundered. "Have any of us fought harder than Harold? The humans were sent to us by the gods. Did you think the gods wouldn't ask something from us?"

Harold felt embarrassed. He put aside his despair. This was no time for brooding about guilt and pride. If Liva still wanted to fight, he would go on fighting beside him.

But what were they going to do? If they waited until the raiders returned to Imeten, and then started attacking slaving parties again, Jemil Min would merely send his army back for more slaughter. After what they had just endured, the Itiji were not going to fight unless Liva offered them something better than that.

Obviously a drawn-out war would never succeed. Everywhere Liva went people begged him not to fight. After enduring the tree-dwellers for centuries, and the ordeals of disease and the elements since they had first evolved, the Itiji did not have the confidence in technology and military power which gave humans and Imetens the patience to pursue far-off, difficult victories. They were not fatalists, but strenuous resistance to pain, death and enslavement was not part of the tradition which shaped their psyches. Most of their philosophies of behavior dealt with the beauty of lives lived within limits which gave them grace and harmony; most of their poems about death urged the hearer to enjoy himself as much as he could.

He found Liva sharing a small, pig-like animal with five of the men who had fought with him during the raid. They were grumbling about the reception they had been getting and discussing the shortcomings of a meal which would normally have fed three.

"I have a proposal," Harold said.

Liva looked up from the foreleg he was gnawing. "I've been wondering when you were going to tell me what you've been thinking about."

"I wanted to think about it very carefully. I think we should attack Imeten."

Liva's companions stopped chewing. Their whiskers wiggled with interest. They still looked to him as a source of miracles.

"I think I can make you weapons which will hurl stones—big stones—from here to the top of that tree. I know I can make you wagons with towers on them as tall as the middle branches. You can run up the inside of the towers and get into the city. You can't climb up there normally, but once you get there you can move around as well as the Imetens. If we can get enough fighters into the city itself, we can hold a portion of it and refuse to leave until they make concessions. We'll have all the advantages of the defense and at the same time we'll be in a place where they can't let us stay."

Liva licked his lips. His five companions made emotional noises.

"How many men will it take?" Liva asked.

"We'll need at least four times eight triple eights. Can you recruit them?"

"How many will live to enter the city?"

"I don't know. Half of us may die in the initial attack."

"You think the few who would be left could hold off the entire Imeten army?"

"If they try to attack us once we're in the city, I think we can kill two of them for every one of us they kill. If they try to wipe us out, they'll lose half their army."

"What if they try to starve us out?"

"If they let us stay that long, Lidris of Drovil will probably hear about it and decide to attack while we're there. Jemil Min won't let that happen. Once he realizes how much of his army he'll have to sacrifice to dislodge us, he'll listen to what we want."

"If the gods are with us," one of the Itiji said.

"If the gods are with us," Harold said.

## XIII

LIVA MOVED among the demoralized communities like a prophet out of the Old Testament. His eyes were focused on the future again.

"The cities of the tree-dwellers throb with cries for help! How can we let people from our own communities—from our own families!—suffer the torments the slaves of the tree-dwellers are enduring every day? Before we had no choice, we were powerless and there was nothing we could do. Now the gods have sent us power. We cannot refuse to fight. The gods gave us the law when they gave us speech. The man who has food will share it with the hungry. No one will ever be abandoned by those who can help him. Forget that law now and the gods will punish us forever. Once the Imetens are conquered by Lidris of Drovil, Lidris will turn the power of five tree-dweller cities against us. *Now* is the time to attack. *Now* the Imetens will fear for their city when they see us."

At the end of two eight-days they had twelve hundred volunteers. When they eliminated the aged, the infirm, and the very young, an army of nine hundred stood ready to be armed. The others would help make weapons and would bring supplies through the Imeten lines after the army was established in the city.

They worked near the mountains at the eastern border of the lands dominated by Ghanis. Liva split the army into groups of forty-eight and scattered them over the forest. While Harold watched in awe, he welded the varied cultures and personalities into a new kind of Itiji community

116

# THE TREE LORD OF IMETEN

—a large fighting community with all the order and discipline of a human or a tree-dweller army, but without the ever-present threat of physical violence the weapon-making species had always used to keep people cooperating. The Itiji might not have a military history, but they did have a political history. Without weapons their leaders had been forced to develop the arts of persuasion. If Jemil Min ever agreed to negotiate, Harold decided, the Imetens would be lucky if they walked away with the clothes they came in.

They worked for fourteen eight-days under constant fear of detection. The first four eight-days Harold and Joanne made tool sets and raised the production per eight-day from fifty shields to seventy. At the end of the period they were outfitting two fighting groups per eight-days. The Itiji were becoming more skillful and had worked out a division of labor which gave the tools to the people who could use them best.

When they started working on the towers and the catapults, a young Itiji suggested a change in plan. Why not mount them on rafts and attack across the river? Advancing across an open, treeless space, they would be safe from the Imetens until they were almost on the city.

They adopted the idea at once. Harold had ben trying to design wheels several times the size of those which the Imetens had installed on the wagons, and he had come to realize exactly how ingenious the first human inventors had been.

They finished the tower in three eight-days. It was a crude structure—a framework made out of lashed-together logs, walls "armored" with smelly hides and a tangle of live, flower-decked vines—but they knew it would do the job. Four meters square and twenty-five meters tall, it was the first building the Itiji had ever possessed. When they practiced running up the interior ramp and storming the middle branches of the trees, they were as delighted as children.

For the catapaults Harold took advantage of the Itiji talent for teamwork. Five Itiji with wooden sandals on their feet jumped off a platform as one man; they landed on a wide crossbar on the long end of the launching arm and the short end snapped up and hurled a ten kilo stone at the upper branches of the trees. It was light artillery, not heavy, but it would batter the Imeten structures along the river front, and it might unnerve the Imetens lined up to stop the assault. He built two and supplemented them with a bow drawn by eight Itiji which could hurl small logs three hundred meters and Imeten spears six hundred meters. Once they were inside the city, the daily havoc wreaked by the bow would be one more argument against a lengthy attempt to starve them to death.

They spent the last four eight-days making two man bows and dartblowers. By the time the last Itiji had put a shield on his back, they had sixty-one missile weapons and several hundred darts and arrows.

They would have had more if Joanne had been able to work faster. She slowed down as soon as she touched a weapon. She couldn't forget she was making something which would eventually kill or mangle a creature who could feel pain and worry about the future.

"Do you want to stay behind?" Harold asked. "It's going to be bad."

She looked at the arrow she was smoothing and bit her lip. "I want to be with you every day we may have left," she said slowly.

He didn't argue with her.

Liva dispatched the army from the mountains group by group over a period of several days. The groups drifted toward the river over routes which ranged over all the coun-

try north of Imeten and Ghanis. Each group carried part
of a dismantled, siege weapon and the routes crossed according to a complicated plan. Every day Liva's group was
supposed to encounter a group which had ended up with
reports from all the other groups.

Harold and Joanne travelled with a group which circled
far to the east. They arrived at the river exactly on schedule, one afternoon after Liva. They were supposed to
work without a break and have the rafts and the siege equipment ready to move right after sunset the next day. If they
set sail just after the first stars rose, according to Harold's
calculations they would arrive at Imeten three hours before
nightfall.

The parts arrived according to the schedule in Liva's
head. As each group finished its part of the job and slipped
into the forest, another group came out of nowhere to take
its place. By dawn they had lashed the rafts together and
erected the framework and half the inside ramp of the tower.

The sun beat on the clearing. They put on hats Joanne had
made out of dried vines and resigned themselves to the taste
of thirst. The sweat poured out of their bodies.

Weariness slowed them down sooner than they had
expected. Evening came again and they still had the top of
the tower to cover and catapult to assemble. Three groups
of Itiji were standing by in the trees.

They ate a cheese fungus dinner and pushed their bodies
back to work. Three hours before dawn the rafts were finally
ready for the river.

Liva howled a signal and the last group of Itiji slipped
from their hiding place and dragged the cumbersome tower to the water. They talked nervously as they pushed the
raft toward the middle of the river through an environment crowded with flesheaters.

Harold dropped the anchors overboard and watched the

Itiji swim back to shore. Joanne was already in her sleeping bag when he looked inside the tower. He laid his own bag on the ramp beside her and dropped on top of it.

He pulled up the anchor just after sunset. The tower slid down the river surrounded by a cloud of insects attracted by the flowers and the Itiji. He took his place by the tiller and the Itiji arranged themselves on each side so the raft would be balanced. The wind hitting the tower made the raft rock as if they were on a choppy sea. The deck was soaked and the Itiji smelled of wet fur.

Joanne sat in front of him on her sleeping bag. For the first time in many eight-days they could watch the stars without trees blocking out most of the sky. She picked out the constellations the refugees used to locate Earth and they stared across the light years at the sun which had given its energy to the planet on which their species had evolved. Even his eyes could enjoy that brilliant point of light when someone told him where it was.

"Someday I'd like to wear glasses just long enough to really see the stars," he said.

She plucked a flower off a vine and brushed it across his hand. "If you ever do, I'd better go hide until you take them off."

She fell asleep sitting with her back against the tower. He put his foot next to hers and listened to the Itiji while he steered. As usual they were expressing their feelings without any shame. "I wish the gods had struck me deaf when Liva spoke," an Itiji on the left side moaned. "I could not ignore suffering women and children. I am more virtuous than I want to be." The others were either frightened but determined, or fanatically convinced the gods were on their side and their human allies were a sure sign victory was inevitable.

"It doesn't matter whether the gods are with us or not,"

one of the frightened Itiji said. "I'm not afraid we'll be defeated. I'm afraid I'm going to die."

As he had learned from his past experiences with them, they could talk freely without losing their self-control.

The dark wall of the forest slipped by. Now and then a big animal rolled in the water near the shore. At his feet Joanne sighed occasionally in her sleep. He kept his eyes open—as did the Itiji, in spite of their talk—and prayed that no monster would suddenly rear up beneath them. The Itiji knew little about the animal life in the river. They had stories about explorers who had ridden fallen logs over parts of it, but in general they stayed near the banks. For swimming they used springs and smaller, clearer streams.

Joanne woke up and they watched the dawn together. The sun worshippers among the Itiji sang their morning prayers. For a moment the river stretched before them like a shining road leading to the immense yellow ball seventy million miles away.

They averted their eyes. In a few minutes the raft had become unbearably hot. Joanne collected all the spears and shields on board and made sunshades for everyone. The Itiji on the other two rafts laid their shields on the catapaults and huddled in a pool of shade at the rear of the deck.

Every now and then wild yaps hailed them from the shore. As each group of Itiji spotted the raft, it let them know the army was hurrying toward the rendezvous.

The sun rose higher. Harold ate a piece of cheese fungus and Joanne took a turn at the tiller so he could rest his arms. On the other rafts the Itiji seemed to be steering the tillers he had constructed for them with no special strain. He felt cramped and hot but the work itself was pleasant.

An hour after noon a keen-eyed Itiji yelled from the bow. Joanne stood up slowly and shaded her eyes. Harold couldn't see it, but he knew it was there, barely visible above the trees—the goddess Niluji and the high wooden tower of Imeten.

## XIV

As THEY approached the city, horns shrieked the alarm. On top of the tower sacrificial smoke drifted toward the sky.

Joanne dismantled the sunshades. Liva and his men rolled into their shields and lay on the deck with their heads pulled in out of the sun. Cries of rage and axiety rose from all three rafts.

"Softer," Liva roared. "They don't know who we are yet. The less they know the better."

The cries faded to a discordant murmur. Joanne crouched beside Harold behind her shield. He pushed on the tiller and the rafts began to drift toward the trees.

He stared intently at the forest. They were still on the eastern edge of the city, a few hundred meters from the place where he planned to run aground. The catapults were creeping up behind him on his river side.

Sunlight flashed on weapons and armor moving in the green blur. Liva raised the hunting song and the other Itiji joined him. Imeten officers shrieked orders. The bodies rushing back and forth made the leaves sway as though a rough wind were shoving the trees.

He turned away from the shore for a moment and then turned back again. A few darts and spears splashed in the water.

Joanne pointed toward the other shore. "They're here! There they are!"

He looked back. He could imagine what they looked like as the black, shielded bodies ran out of the forest and plunged into the river. In the city hundreds of voices screamed. Pans clattered for order.

"How many?" he asked. "Are they all there?"

"They're still coming," Joanne said.

Liva was singing at the top of his lungs. He stood up and looked back at Harold with his savage mouth wide open.

"The hunt is on! The quarry is at bay! Sharp claws gallop toward the kill!"

On the shore a big animal lumbered into the river and swam away from the din with its hump and its head above the water. They were now about a hundred and fifty meters offshore and about two hundred meters from the landing place he wanted near the middle of the city. The catapults had turned and were moving in beside him.

The Itiji in the water sang the hunting song as they swam. The first group was already in the middle of the river.

A few darts landed about twenty meters from the raft. Harold untied his shield with one hand and held it between his body and the shore.

"You'd better get in the tower, Jo. We're almost in range."

She pressed his hand and stepped inside the door. Liva and his men raced up the ramp to man the dartblowers mounted in the tower.

On the catapult rafts the launching team climbed onto the shielded platform on the bow. The synchronizer crouched behind the low wall beside the launching arm and watched the shore. The first rock had been sitting in the pouch on the short end of the arm ever since they had left the rendezvous. The two men working the tiller with their teeth had the anchors placed where they could kick them overboard as soon as the synchronizer ordered.

The Itiji leading the swimmers paddled toward the rear of the tower. He waved at them and the leader sang a greeting. Their shields made them look like long black turtles.

Joanne pointed across the river. "They're still coming out of the forest. It looks like they all made it."

The Itiji swam up to the raft and pressed their foreheads against the padded rear log. Darts dropped into the water on all sides. A spear crashed into Harold's shield and jarred his arm. He looked up at the trees and saw the first ranks of the Imetens waiting for him in the leaves.

The second group of Itiji arrived at the raft. The first group climbed out of the river one by one and ran up the ramp. Joanne stopped each one at the door and made sure his shield and his weapons were in order. The deck ran with water from their dripping bodies.

The catapaults had dropped anchor. Harold glanced at them just as a perfectly synchronized team jumped off the platform. The rock shot up at a steep angle. For a moment everyone in the river and the trees seemed to be hushed by the sight. The rock hung for an instant over the front ranks of the Imetens and then it crashed through the trees. The Itiji cheered. Imetens shrieked. The branches swayed as officers fought to get their men under control.

Darts flew out of the tower at the trees. Another rock rose toward the city and dropped on the Imetens.

Branches scraped against the top of the tower. More Itiji dragged themselves onto the raft and ran noisily up the ramp. Darts and spears rained on the river. Imetens charged along the branches to meet the invaders. Somewhere at the edge of Harold's consciousness an Itiji wailed in pain. A tree-dweller body dropped through the leaves. The first blood flowed on the dark water of the river.

Every Itiii climbing aboard seemed to have an Imeten missile dangling in his shield. Harold's right side was soaked from the water they left on his clothes as they brushed past. They were streaming up the ramp faster than Joanne could examine them. A few stopped to have her adjust shields which had slipped during the swim. The rest ran past her with the hunting song ringing in their throats.

A spear quivered in the deck near the base of Harold's shield. An Itiji halfway out of the water screamed in his ear and slipped back into the river with a spear piercing his shield and blood gushing out of his mouth.

He looked up. Imetens were crowding onto the branches near the top of the tower. They were swinging their maces at the dartblower tubes sticking out of the sides and shoving their spears through the walls and stabbing at random. Darts flew at them from the tower at arms' length range. Spearmen wrapped their legs around the branches directly above the deck and hurled their shafts straight down with all the force a strong tree-dweller arm could add to the planet's powerful gravity.

Harold crouched behind his shield with one hand on the tiller. Another Itiji screamed as a spear plunged through his shield. Ropes dropped from the trees and a gang of boarders began to descend on the raft.

He let go of the tiller and stood up with his sword in one hand and his shield in the other. The raft was pointed at the bank, and the Itiji were still pushing it. "Back up the ramp," he yelled at Joanne. "They're coming aboard."

Her eyes widened. She stepped back and disappeared into the darkness.

The Itiji who had just crawled out of the water howled their anger at the Imetens climbing down the ropes. They rallied around him and he waved the next group up the ramp. In the back of his mind he heard another rock dropping through the trees. He pointed his sword at the sky.

"The gods are with us! Gliad! Gliad!"

A swarm of screaming Imetens dropped on the deck. Harold blocked a mace with his shield and slashed a spearman's wrist. Spearmen jumped on the Itiji and tried to plunge their shafts through the shields. Claws raked at flesh. Itiji and Imetens fell struggling into the water. In seconds wounded of both species were being trampled underfoot.

The raft lurched as the Itiji shoved it against the bank. The door in the tower fell open and Itiji shoved the landing ramps at the trees. The first assault party charged onto the branches. Darts and spears thudded on shields. The warcries of the Imetens mingled with the hunting song of the Itiji. The Imetens in the forward ranks braced themselves to meet the charge.

Harold pushed an Imeten into the water with his shield. Behind his back the Itiji continued to climb on the deck and run up the ramp.

"We've landed! Attack! Go! The gods are with us!"

He stared blankly at the remains of the slaughter on the raft. The last Imeten in the boarding party had just gone to the deck under the fangs of an Itiji. The wounded and dying of both species were writhing on the deck and struggling to keep afloat in the water.

Harold looked back at the river. More than half the Itiji had gone up the ramp. Above him a stream of black demons was shooting out of the tower. The landing ramps were firmly in place and the first rush of the Itiji seemed to have carried them into the front lines of the Imetens. Above the din of the battle the clear voices of the Itiji were communicating steadily. The fighting community adjusted to the changing situation as if the five hundred individuals in the trees were a single organism. If he had listened carefully he could have learned the exact location of every Itiji.

He crouched behind his shield and sent the Itiji up the ramp with shouts of encouragement. The hunting song carried good news. The forward eights of the Imetens were falling back. The Itiji had established a perimeter. The rocks from the catapult were damaging houses and bridges and creating a turmoil in the rear of the battle. The two-man missile launchers were sending death streaking toward the unshielded bodies of the Imetens.

He followed the last Itiji up the ramp. Joanne picked up her shield as he trudged toward her, and they climbed side by side. It was a harder climb for two legs than for four. Her fingers touched his knuckles and he put his sword in its sheath and squeezed her shoulder. He couldn't see her face in the darkness. She pressed herself against him and he moved away so that the blood on his legs wouldn't rub off on her.

"Are you all right?" he asked.

"I'll be fine. Don't worry about me. Just try to stay alive."

Liva was crouching below the door. They knelt beside him behind their shields and looked out. In the shadows under the leaves the two armies were struggling only two trees from the tower. Crowded onto the narrow bridges and the thick branches, the Itiji were pushing forward in all three dimensions. The last Itiji to leave the tower were still only a few paces from the ramp. Everywhere they looked they could glimpse savage individual combats through the openings in the trees. The branches shook beneath the movements of several hundred struggling bodies. It was the slaughter on the raft all over again—multiplied several hundred times.

"Where should I go?" Harold asked.

"We're in trouble on the left," Liva said. "I think they've

started a counter-attack. The trees are thick there and we're being attacked from above."

"How many of us have they killed?"

Liva's head turned from side to side. He was listening to the hunting song as they talked. "I've counted eight times eight. I think we've killed four to five times eight Imetens."

He got his bow and his quiver out of a weapon chest in the back of the tower. When he returned to the door he bent over behind his shield and touched Joanne's hand.

"I'll be back," he said.

She looked up at him. Her eyes glistened. "Be careful."

He stepped onto the landing ramp and ran toward the battle line. The Itiji crowded on the branches moved aside to let him pass. He used their shields for handholds and they dug their claws into the bark to give him firmer support. Imetens screamed his name. Darts and spears flew at him from the upper branches.

He ran across a bridge toward a clot of struggling bodies. Several Imetens swung at him suddenly on ropes. He hacked at them as they came by, catching blows and missiles on his shield, and rallied the Itiji holding the bridgehead with a bellow.

"Stand by me! Stay with me! Back them into the ocean!"

Snipers blew darts at him from every direction. An assault party of two double eights swung at the bridgehead, screaming for the traitor's life. He retreated into an abandoned house and fought back with his bow and the aid of three two-man teams. The Itiji who had followed him across the bridge were forced to retreat. More Imetens assaulted the house. Spears stabbed at him through the flimsy roof. The Itiji fighting at his side called on the gods for mercy and bewailed their fate—and aimed their weapons as cooly and lethally as people who had been using weapons all their lives.

# THE TREE LORD OF IMETEN

A small army of Itiji rushed across the bridge and leaped on the Imetens. Liva had sent reinforcements. The Imetens backed up and Harold bellowed and came out of the house with his sword swinging.

By nightfall they were firmly established in the city. They had pushed inward one hundred meters from the river and they had strong positions at all but the highest levels.

They worked all night, tearing down bridges and establishing bow and dartblower teams where they could cover the few approaches the Imetens would be able to use. The giant bow was set up close to the perimeter and the catapults were anchored beside the tower.

Harold slept in the tower, near the small fire he had built so that Joanne could see while she gave the wounded the extra help only a pair of hands could provide. Even the wails of the wounded couldn't keep him awake. He slept from the moment he dropped on his sleeping bag until Liva woke him up half an hour before dawn.

He listened to the news while he ate a piece of cheese fungus. A small party on the ground had been doing what it could for the wounded who had fallen from the trees, and the leader had reported that the party had stumbled across thirty-two Imeten casualties. Liva's final count of their own casualties had been one hundred and six dead and twenty-two seriously wounded.

"There must be more Imetens down there," Harold said. "They were working in the dark. The Imetens can keep themselves in the trees better than our wounded can, too. I think we should add at least another double eight to our estimate of the Imeten casualties."

"That means we've killed about eight to ten eights," Liva said.

Harold nodded. Discussions like this still made him uncomfortable. "And yesterday they were on the defensive. Today we'll reverse the ratio."

## XV

THE IMETENS attacked through the mists of dawn. The horn on the great tower shrieked once and the first assault parties swung toward the Itiji lines. Groups of two and three double eights raced down the branches with their spears lowered.

A volley of darts and arrows sailed at their unshielded bodies. The Itiji raised the hunting song as if it were a hymn of thanks and braced themselves to meet the charge.

All day long the Imetens hammered at the Itiji lines. Harold posted himself in the center and threw his bow and his hand weapons into the battle wherever the hunting song told him he was most needed. In the early afternoon an assault party broke through a weak point and charged the tower itself. They were stopped before they stormed the entrance only because Joanne picked up the mace Harold had given her and added her hands and her shield to the struggles of the handful of Itiji left to guard the wounded. When Harold arrived with a rescue force, most of the Itiji who had been with her were dead and she was fighting in desperate silence on the landing ramp, her hair falling around her face and three Itiji standing with her against twelve Imetens. The reinforcements rushed in with Harold in the lead and in seconds the Imetens were surrounded and killed.

# THE TREE LORD OF IMETEN

He didn't see her when he recovered from the frenzy of the skirmish. He found her sitting in the rear of the tower, staring at her mace. He made sure she wasn't hurt and then he touched her shoulder and returned to the battle.

At the end of the day eighty-six Itiji had been killed, and about a hundred and fifty Imetens. The Itiji raised their heads to the gods and sang a hymn of thanks.

"They've lost one man in every double eight," Harold said. "Four more days like today and Jemil Min can ask Lidris to come and be High Warrior."

For supper the Itiji ate the provisions they had carried with them and the few fish which the foraging parties had splashed out of the water. When they settled down to sleep on their uncomfortable perches, complaints about hunger could be heard on every side.

Liva's morning howl roused the camp. As the light filtered through the trees they braced themselves for another onslaught. The Itiji trembled with eagerness at their posts.

The last wisps of dew rose from the foliage. The Imetens remained in their places. Only screams of command and an occasional dart told the invaders their enemy was still there.

They got out the long arrows piled in the tower and put the big bow to work. The heavy missiles shot through the trees and the Itiji cheered every time they heard the scream of dying Imetens or the sound of a house being smashed. Down below the catapults lifted the few small rocks they could find near the landing point.

"The Warriors cower before their superiors," Itiji, who knew the Imeten language, howled across the lines. "Their slaves foul their city. They cringe before our claws. Smell the fear of the Warriors. The Itiji have defeated them. The Itiji

131

have trampled on them. They will be the slaves of slaves. The gods have spoken—and the Warriors have fled."

No one answered. In their posts hidden in the leaves, the Imeten officers kept their men under control.

The Itiji began to grow restless. "They're going to starve us," voices wailed. "They won't attack. We've failed."

Liva moved among the community and reaffirmed his faith in Harold's judgment of the Imeten character. After one of those discussions which drove Harold mad with impatience, five eights of the army stayed at their posts, and the other three eights spent the day foraging for fish, birds' eggs, and whatever the Imetens had left behind. As soon as night came a few hunting parties slipped out of the city on the ground. The Itiji went to bed with half-filled bodies but they obviously weren't going to starve for another day or two.

On the morning of the third day a voice called to them across the lines.

"Itiji! Slaves! The High Warrior sends his orders. Hear and obey. Surrender and we will let you live. Give us the two-legs who gave you weapons and we will let you live. Disobey and you will starve to death here—and we will return to your country and punish your wives and children."

Liva hurried down the crowded branches to the front of the enclave. All around him black bodies were wiggling with emotion. Teeth were bared for combat.

"Imeten! Cursed of the gods! Hear and obey! Free every Itiji in your city. Swear you will never take another Itiji slave. Swear you will never enter our country again without our permission. As punishment for what you did to our wives and children, make shields and weapons for every Itiji north of the river. The gods have sent us and the gods will keep us here. We will kill and destroy without mercy. For every Itiji you killed when you invaded our land, two Imetens will die. We will destroy your army. We will leave you defenseless before your enemies. The gods have spoken! Obey the gods!"

The Itiji howled the hunting song. Darts and arrows flew toward the Imeten lines.

That night a foraging party came down the river on a raft loaded with food. Harold and Liva met them at the bottom of the tower and listened soberly to the leader's report. The foraging parties on the other side of the river had been doing their best to reach the city. The Imetens were patrolling the shore for half a day's walk in both directions.

"We stole the raft from Ghanis," the leader said. "We didn't have shields but they weren't expecting us. After this everything you get will have to be swum across the river. I'm supposed to ask you if that's what you want us to do. If it is, we'll do it."

They escorted him to the top of the tower and Liva supervised the distribution of the food. By dividing it up very carefully he managed to make it feed one in eight.

"Stay another day or two," Liva told the foragers. "We won't ask the others to swim the river unless we have to. Harold is right: Jemil Min may know he shouldn't attack, but sooner or later his enemies in the city will force him to. Already some would-be High Warrior must be muttering he would drive us out of here in a day if he were the leader."

Hope faded minutes after sunrise. By nightfall the Itiji were restless again. For the first time a few voices suggested the community should leave the city and try to fight its way through the Imeten patrols.

Harold stood on the landing platform and listened to the arguments criss-crossing in the darkness. A full scale community debate had erupted. Liva and about a hundred others were arguing for patience and a few were insisting they should leave. Most of the rest wanted to attack.

# THE TREE LORD OF IMETEN

*It's been three days! . . . They aren't going to attack. . . .
Harold was wrong. . . . Attack, Liva, attack! . . . Attack or
leave! . . . .*

Liva stalked out of the darkness and marched into the
tower. He leaped on the wall with a roar and raked it with
his claws.

"How the gods must laugh at us! No wonder we're
slaves!"

Harold stepped off the ramp. Joanne glanced at him across
the dimly-lit room. The wounded Itiji lying on the floor wailed
fitfully.

"We have to attack," Liva said. "We can't wait, Harold.
If we don't act, by tomorrow some of them will start leaving. We came here to kill Imetens—by the sun and the
trees, let's do it!"

Harold stared at the darkness outside the door. His shoulders felt heavy. Now he knew why human generals had
rarely been young men in their early twenties.

"It will be as bad as the landing," he said. "It may even
be worse."

"If that's what the gods want, it will have to be."

"You don't think you can hold the community together
another day?"

"They'll stay if we attack. That's what we're like. That's
why we had to come here. Are they wrong? It's been three
days!"

Harold listened to the Itiji arguing. The Imetens must
have at least one man who could understand what they
were saying. By now Jemil Min knew they were beginning
to crumble.

He braced himself. "We'll do whatever the community
wants," he said. "It's up to them. We can't do anything they
don't want to do."

## XVI

At dawn the Itiji plunged across the bridges at the spears of the eights drawn up to meet them. Once again the branches shook beneath the feet of hundreds of struggling creatures. Blood spattered on the green. *Bear the panting body down,* wailed the hunting song. *Scrape your claws on flesh. . . . Crush the throat beneath your fangs. . . .*

At the end of the day a hundred more Itiji were dead. They had pushed into the city another fifty meters and they had killed approximately seventy Imetens. When they raised their voices to the gods of night, they sang the prayer of mourning.

Harold slept with one hand touching Joanne. The noise of the battle clamored in his brain. He could still feel the heat and the grime on his body when he woke at dawn and went out to push forward again.

Black, swift bodies charged relentlessly across the branches. Imeten faces grimaced at him over his shield and died with his sword in their bodies. His mouth burned with the thirst of exertion. His spirit rose and fell with the hunting song and the surge of the battle.

He ran across the treacherous branches as if he were drunk or insane. Time after time the first wave in a charge died to a man and killed every Imeten who had dared to stand his ground. The hunting song reported minor epics on every side. His name came to him through the frenzy as if the voices of the generations of Itiji who would sing of his deeds were hailing him across the centuries. *Harold has*

135

*killed six. . . . Harold has held a bridge alone. . . . Harold has cleared a way on the left. . . . Follow Harold. . . . Fight like Harold. . . .*

Both sides were reeling when the day ended. They broke apart almost by mutual consent. The Itiji had advanced another hundred meters and nearly a hundred Imetens had been killed or seriously wounded. Ninety-two Itiji had hailed the sun for the last time.

They sang the hymn of thanks. Parched voices promised the Imetens they would do better tomorrow.

Harold dropped among the Itiji sprawled on the landing ramp and ate his cheese fungus. He was lying half-asleep when a guard at the front of the enclave called Liva's name.

"What is it?" Liva asked.

"Come forward. Bring Harold."

"What is it?"

"Come forward. Hurry."

Liva stood up. Harold raised his head and they looked at each other. "We'd better go," Liva said.

Joanne came to the door of the tower. She had been working with the wounded since early afternoon. "What is it, Harold?"

"I don't know. We're going to see."

They picked their way along the branches. Liva went first and Harold stayed on his tail and trusted his life to the night vision of the Itiji. Itiji moved aside with many grumbles, and an occasional apology when they remembered what they had done during the day.

"What is it?" voices muttered. "Are they coming to talk?"

"Pray," Liva said. "Hope."

The guard was posted at the front end of a bridge. Liva went forward into the darkness alone. Harold looked up at the sky and prayed to whatever gods might be.

Two shadows crept toward him across the bridge. The one in front was an Imeten walking on all fours.

"Be quiet," Liva whispered. "Don't talk until we're well in the rear."

The Imeten stepped off the bridge. Harold raised his shield and stepped aside to let him pass. He fell in behind Liva. They crossed another bridge and stopped on a branch far from any listening ears. The Imeten pulled himself semi-erect on a vine.

"Welcome," Liva said. "Consider yourself our guest. You are as safe and protected as an Itiji in his own community."

"I'd better be," the Imeten said. "Betray me and we'll drive you off the face of the world."

It was Nimenlej. A surge of excitement blotted out Harold's weariness. He stood behind Liva with his shield raised and let the Itiji do the talking.

"I have a message from the High Warrior," Nimenlej said. "Obey and you will live. Disobey and you will all die. The gods have indicated Itiji are not to be slaves any longer. The gods have their ways and only fools defy them. Tomorrow Harold Lizert will appear before the High Warrior and his Council and swear he was sent by the gods and the gods want us to free our Itiji slaves. If he can swear this is true, all Itiji now enslaved will be freed. Itiji will be fighters, not slaves. From now on you will fight beside the Warriors of Imeten whenever the High Warrior commands."

Harold smiled to himself. If he had had less faith in Imeten honor, he would have suspected a trap. As it was, he was amused by the way Nimenlej presented all his proposals right at the start. Obviously bargaining was not a part of tree-dweller culture.

On the other hand, the High Warrior obviously knew how to engineer social change. The mysterious representative of a new species was supposed to masquerade as the messenger of the gods. The radical innovation was to be justified by tradition.

"Warriors need shields and weapons," Liva said. "Will you make them for us?"

"We will send you slaves from the cities of Ghanis and Drovil. Whenever the High Warrior calls for you, you will appear before him fully armed. Every male Itiji will fight for us. Any male Itiji who disobeys a call to arms will be punished for desertion."

Liva turned his head to the left and stared at the darkness. After a minute Nimenlej began to wiggle restlessly.

"Why does Harold have to appear before the High Warrior?" Liva asked.

"The High Warrior commands it."

"Will you swear he won't be harmed? He won't be punished for desertion?"

"He will not be harmed or punished in any way. I swear it."

Liva lapsed into silence again. Harold started to speak and then stopped himself.

"Are you willing to do this, Harold?" Liva asked.

"Yes."

"Then I think we'll accept. When will the Council meet?"

"In the morning," Nimenlej said. "I will escort him myself."

## XVII

HE MARCHED THROUGH Imeten with Nimenlej and a triple eight to guard him. Spectators crowded every branch as he climbed toward the tower. Behind him in the enclave the

Itiji were beginning to respond to the first scent of victory with songs of love and pleasure. Joanne had looked almost happy.

"The High Warrior hasn't told the Council you're coming," Nimenlej said. "Don't speak until he tells you to. Keep your hands off your weapons. If any fighting starts, be ready to leave as soon as I tell you to. I'll protect your retreat. I have sworn you will not be harmed—if anything happens to you, it will happen after I'm dead."

Harold nodded. "How far should I run?" he asked.

"I'll tell you when the time comes."

The triple eight paused on the bridge in front of the tower. Two guards flanked him and he followed Nimenlej into the council room.

Heads snapped up. Warriors screamed questions at Jemil Min. At the far end of the left row of couches, a priest rose to his hands and knees on his log and pointed with one arm. "Traitor! Deserter! The gods will punish you! *The gods demand your life!*"

"He is here as my guest!" the High Warrior screamed. "He is not a prisoner. Silence! Hear him! I have sworn he will not be harmed. Blindness and pain for the man who touches him."

Harold stood stiffly erect behind his shield. The screaming voices racked his nerves more than the din of battle. Angry eyes darted from him to the High Warrior.

The priest shook his fist. Harold couldn't see his face well enough to be sure, but he thought it was the Great Priest himself. "What have I lived to see? The High Warrior of Imeten has sworn to protect a deserter! The gods tremble with rage!"

Half the warriors in the room rose on their logs. Nimenlej jerked his mace off his belt. The two guards looked around the room and pulled out their spears.

# THE TREE LORD OF IMETEN

"Tell them your tale," Jemil Min screamed. "Tell them what you swore to Nimenlej Lumin."

Harold pointed his right arm at the roof. "Hear and obey," he screamed in Imeten. "Hear the will of the gods!"

Every Warrior in the room was wiggling with emotion. A few had even lowered their heads as if they were crouching to spring. He spoke as fast as his lungs could rasp the air through his throat.

"The gods told me to leave my country and go across the mountains to Imeten but they did not tell me why. As I was marching toward Ghanis with Nimenlej, the goddess Niluji appeared before me. The Itiji have found new favor in the eyes of the gods, she said. The gods prize the Warriors of Imeten, too, and wish to see Lidris of Drovil humbled. Lidris tries to rule more than the gods gave him. Let the Warriors of Imeten and the Itiji who will follow you be the weapons of our vengeance. Lead the Itiji against Imeten that the Warriors may learn our will. All Itiji slaves must be freed. From this day forth the Itiji are fighters, not slaves. They will make war by the side of the Warriors against the enemies of the gods. If the Warriors obey, their city will endure forever. If they disobey they will be destroyed. Imeten will be buried in the mold beneath the trees. Hear and obey."

He lowered his hand. Several mouths opened to speak. He had learned enough about tree-dweller expressions to know they would have killed him then and there if they had dared.

Jemil Min's eyes flickered around the room. "Do you swear this is true?"

Harold raised his hand again. "I swear by all the immortal—"

"Judge what he says by what you know of the gods," the Great Priest screamed. "The gods have raised the Warriors

140

above all other creatures. Would the Itiji let us enslave them if the gods meant them to be free? He insults the goddess! He fouls her city. He will bring her wrath upon us!"

A Warrior pounded on his log. "What can he swear by? He swore to serve us and he deserted. He insults every god! Jemil Min has brought him here to trick us into accepting defeat!"

Jemil Min's back arched. He turned toward the Warrior who had dared to say such a thing in his presence. His dart-blowers raised their tubes to their lips.

"Kill him!" A Warior shrieked. "Kill the deserter!"

"Avenge the goddess!"

"Drown the slaves in the river!"

Jemil Min slapped his log. "Silence! Hear and obey! Silence!"

The screams crescendoed. Warriors shook their fists at Harold and Jemil Min. Nimenlej brandished his mace above his shoulder.

"Insects!" Jemil Min said. "The gods are giving you a prize. Lidris is doomed."

"Slaves are slaves," the Great Priest chanted. "Warriors are Warriors. The gods gave the law to your fathers. Obey the gods."

"Give us a leader," a Warrior screamed, "and we'll see what the gods want. Do the gods want Jemil Min?"

Jemil Min turned on his log. His hand moved toward his spear. The warrior who had flung the challenge arched his back and reached for his own spear. They stared at each other across the room.

Nimenlej looked back at Harold. "Run! Go all the way back to the Itiji!"

Every Warrior in the room was reaching for his weapons. The gods were about to speak.

Harold's brain reeled. Jemil Min must have brought him

here out of desperation. The victory was an illusion. The Itiji had suffered and died for nothing. They had come to make Jemil Min negotiate and instead they had merely destroyed his authority. He had led them into a massacre.

He gripped the hilt of his sword. Who came first? Joanne? Himself? The three races who would someday occupy this planet? The Itiji who had died because they had trusted his judgment and believed their sacrifice would accomplish something?

The music of the hunting song rose and fell in his mind. He threw back his head. His voice filled the room.

"I was sent by the gods," he screamed. "Let the gods show you. Pick the best Warrior you have to fight me."

## XVIII

"How CAN YOU fight in the grid?" Liva wailed. "You were made to fight on the ground. Would you fight a flesh-eating fish in the river?"

"I've fought the Imetens in the trees ever since we got here," Harold said. "Most of the time I've even been outnumbered. I've got a reasonable chance. If I didn't think I could win, I wouldn't have challenged them. I want to live as much as you do."

"You've been fighting on bridges and branches. The grid is made just for them—for leaping and swinging. You're risking everything we've accomplished on one fight."

"It's our only hope. Jemil Min was about to go down. If he falls, he'll be replaced by somebody who won't surrender until we're all dead and half the Imeten army has been wiped out. If I lose, you can go back to the forest and keep on fighting. You don't have to keep any promises I make. We don't have anything to lose! If I don't do this we may as well retreat today. Every Itiji who's died here will have died for nothing."

Liva rose on his hind legs and broke a branch with a savage blow of his forepaws. "You'll be killed! You'll die! What will we do without you?"

Harold looked across the enclave at the Itiji peering at him through the leaves. The community was relatively quiet; murmured voices were carrying everything he and Liva said to the furthest outpost.

"You can go on fighting," he said. "You have the tools now to make your own weapons. You've proved you can meet the tree-dwellers in open battle and hurt them as much as they hurt you. You don't need me. If I survive, then all the people who will die if you go on fighting the Imetens will survive with me. If I die—make them wish I hadn't."

Joanne was standing in the entrance to the tower. He turned around and walked toward her across the landing ramp. He hadn't talked to her alone yet.

She fell into his arms. "Oh, Harold—"

"Let's go below."

He turned her around and they walked down the ramp in silence. Behind them the Itiji were beginning to talk again. Already he could hear wails of terror and despair.

She fell into his arms again as soon as they were alone on the raft. Her shoulders quivered. He held her face against his chest and patted her back.

"It's no worse than what we've already been through, Jo. We could both have died anytime. If I win, we've won everything. It'll be all over."

"I love you! I don't want you to die!"

Terrible sobs shook her body. He looked down at her and wished he could leave her now and stay away from her until it was all over. He had been dreading this scene since he had left the council room.

"I've made up my mind. Don't spoil whatever we've got left. This is no worse than it's been since we first decided to help them. Do you want a world run by people like those animals we left in charge back on the plateau? I want us to have children someday—do you want them to grow up in the kind of mess we made on Earth? Men have been doing things like this since they started walking on two legs. It's the way the world is. Don't fail me now. You've been a good wife—hold on a little longer."

She stopped sobbing. Her arms slid around his chest and she squeezed him as hard as she could. He stroked her hair and rocked back and forth.

"What do you want to do?" she said.

He looked up at the tower. From here the trees and the river looked deserted. There was plenty of shade and the waves would rock them while they slept. They could even bathe in the river water.

"I'll ask Liva to have them leave us alone here. We'll do whatever we want to do. You need a rest more than I do."

They woke up just after dark. He knelt behind her on the deck and stroked her hair and they looked at the stars together.

"I've got two things to say," he said. "I wouldn't mention them if they weren't important to me."

"Go ahead. I'll be all right."

"If I don't live, you may want to go back to the settlement again sooner or later. If you do—if you have any children tell them about me. I always wanted to have children."

She caught her breath. He held onto her shoulders and waited.

"If I have any children by anybody," she said, "you'll be their father."

He swallowed. "No one could have acted better than you have. You've been a miracle. You've been everything a woman should be."

"Oh, Harold—"

He held her while she cried. This time he didn't argue with her.

Liva's morning howl roused them shortly after dawn. Harold washed in the river and they ate a cheese fungus breakfast in silence. They had both said everything they had to say.

Liva came down the ramp alone. "Did you sleep well?"

"I haven't felt this good in several eight-days," Harold said.

"Nimenlej is waiting for you at the bridge where we met him the first time. Do you still want to do this?"

He hooked his mace on his belt and strapped his sword on his back Imeten style. "I've made up my mind, Liva. Please don't argue with me."

"I won't. I argued with you yesterday because I like you. You're doing the right thing, Harold. Go with the gods."

The Itiji shouted with one voice when they stepped onto the landing ramp. The hunting song soared above the enclave. He squeezed Joanne's hand and stepped forward. Murmurs of encouragement and good wishes followed him as he advanced toward the front lines. Soft paws touched his hands.

Nimenlej was waiting for him with a triple eight. An Imeten handed him a spear in a sheath and he examined it and strapped it on his back next to his sword.

"The gods are waiting," Nimenlej screamed. "Follow me."

He waved at the Itiji standing on the other side of the

bridge. Nimenlej stepped in front of him and the triple eight fell in with half the men in front of them and half behind.

"The gods go with you," the Itiji shouted. "Gliad! Gliad!"

He followed Nimenlej up a ladder nailed to a tree trunk. They climbed toward the top of the city. Imeten soldiers peered at them from their posts hidden in the leaves. Most of the city's inhabitants were waiting for them at the grid, and the noise of the crowd came to him as he climbed.

"The gods have chosen Lujinet Nin Tujetu," Nimenlej said. "He's young and he's very fast. He was the Warrior everyone talked about after the last Choosing."

"Has he fought in the grid before?"

"Not since he became a Warrior."

"How would you fight him?"

"Let him attack you. He's fast but he gets tired fast, too. Wear him down."

They stepped off the ladder and trotted out of the shade on a bridge which spanned the top of the grid. Sunlight beat on his face. The crowd below screamed insults. He gripped the handrails and tried not to look down.

Jemil Min and the Great Priest were both holding themselves semi-erect on a platform at the end of the bridge. A Warrior was crouching in front of them and the Great Priest was making passes with his free hand and haranguing the statue of the goddess.

Nimenlej crouched in front of his superiors and slapped wood. The Great Priest lowered his eyes from the goddess.

"Go!" Jemil Min ordered.

Nimenlej led his men down a ladder. Harold rested his hand on his mace and met the eyes of the two Imetens.

"The gods know we are here," the Great Priest said. "Go to your places."

The young Warrior screamed a battle cry. The crowd

cheered and he jumped off the platform and swung hand over hand toward the south side of the grid.

Harold walked back to the middle of the bridge and knelt carefully on the narrow footboard. He stuck his hand under the handrail and gripped a top rung with both hands. For a moment he had to look straight down through the framework.

He pulled in a deep breath to make himself relax. His legs slid off the bridge and his feet found the next rung down. He edged toward the north side of the grid with his arms wrapped around the upper rung. The vertical distance between rungs was a little less than the height of his shoulder; the horizontal distance was a strenuous jump across a drop which would kill him if he missed or fell short.

The sun burned the back of his neck. The crowd screamed at him to hurry. He reached the side and crawled down an upright until he was at the traditional starting place five rungs below the top. Across the grid Lujinet Nin hung carelessly by one hand. Spectators grimaced at him from branches an easy leap from his back.

He wiped the sweat off his face. The horn on the tower shrieked twice. The crowd wiggled with excitement.

Lujinet Nin followed up the grid hand over hand. Harold inched toward the center, clutching the rung near his shoulder with both hands.

He stopped two uprights in. Lujinet Nin swung two uprights to the west and climbed on top of the grid. The spidery silhouette stalked toward him on all fours across the glare of the sun.

He gripped an upright with one hand and shielded his eyes with the other. Lujinet Nin stopped directly overhead and pulled his spear out of its sheath.

Harold drew his own spear. They stared at each other through the framework with their weapons poised above their shoulders. The sun flamed in Harold's eyes.

He dropped his head and looked up through his eyebrows. Lujinet Nin's arm descended.

He threw his own spear and twisted toward the upright. He jumped off the rung he was standing on and grabbed at the rung which crossed it. His fingers clutched for a handhold. His feet scrambled on the lower rung. Lujinet Nin screamed a battle cry and swung toward him through the framework.

Lujinet Nin jumped at the rung opposite him and drew his sword in mid-air. His three-fingered hand curled around the wood. He kicked off the bottom rung and swung across the void and stabbed.

Harold parried. The strength of Lujinet Nin's arm made him gasp. His sword twisted in his grip. Lujinet Nin fell back and swung at him again. Their swords clanged. Lujinet Nin fell back and rested for a moment on his rung.

"I was sent by the gods," Harold screamed. "The priest has sent you to your doom."

A strange expression flickered across Lujinet Nin's face. It was the same look of awe and fear Harold had seen yesterday on the faces of most of the Imetens in the council room. Would he have offered to fight in the grid if he hadn't been sent by the gods?

He gestured with his sword. His arm still ached from the impact of the last parry. "The gods are waiting for you. Come!"

Lujinet Nin stepped sideways. His long toes curled around the rung as if they were fingers. He stepped onto the rung which crossed the one he was standing on and crept around the frame with his sword pointed at his adversary. Hate and fear twisted his face. In all the fighting he had done, Harold had never seen an Imeten look more savage.

He waited with his sword raised. Sweat dripped into his eyes and he wiped his face on the sleeve of his sword arm.

Lujinet Nin stepped onto the rung he was standing on and took one step forward. The point of the Imeten's sword shot at his face.

He parried. Lujinet Nin's sword slid past his blade and he stepped back. Lujinet Nin stabbed again. The upright pressed against his back and he twisted around it and edged backward. Step by step the Imeten backed him toward the center of the grid. The sword poked at him relentlessly. Lujinet Nin's arm forced it past his strongest parries. Retreat was his only defense.

He braced himself between the rungs and parried with all his strength. Their blades pressed together. His overdeveloped muscles strained against muscles adapted to this gravity. They glared at each other across their upraised arms. He gathered his courage and prepared to risk everything on an Imeten tactic: a two-handed slash as he dropped off the rung. With luck he would grab a handhold before he hit the ground.

Lujinet Nin shrieked. His body shifted away from the rungs and he dropped. Harold's sword banged against the rung above his head. He lurched forward from the waist and his feet slipped on the wood. The crowd screamed. Lujinet Nin grabbed the rung he was standing on and stabbed upward at his exposed stomach.

He parried awkwardly. Iron rasped on iron. Lujinet Nin's sword pressed toward his hip. He lifted his front foot off the rung and stepped on Lujinet Nin's hand with his heel.

Lujinet Nin grimaced. His sword arm faltered. He dropped another rung and looked up with bared teeth. "Slave! Insect!" He sheathed his sword and swung away through the framework. Again he climbed toward the sky.

Harold watched through half-closed eyes. The sun beat on his face. He sheathed his sword and hung onto the framework with both hands. His left arm felt cramped.

Lujinet Nin stalked him across the top of the grid. He drew his sword and positioned himself against an upright. He had learned enough about this kind of fighting to know what to expect next.

The Imeten hung above the grid like a black bird of prey. He shrieked a prayer at the goddess and dropped through the framework with one hand raised above his head and the butt of his sword pressed against his hip.

Harold raised his sword. Lujinet Nin twisted away from the point and stabbed as he fell past. Harold parried and his sword shrieked against the free-falling blade.

Fingers closed on the wrist of his sword arm. The plummeting body pulled his hand down. A sudden wrench jerked his fingers off the framework.

He fell toward Lujinet Nin's grimacing face. His free hand clutched for a hold. Rungs banged his legs. Fire ran through his body as his glands and his nervous system reacted to the alien gravity with an overdose of hormones and nerve impulses. He screamed in panic.

His sword slipped out of his hand. Lujinet Nin's fingers slid off his wrist. He twisted frantically and clutched at the framework with both hands.

His left hand closed around a rung. His legs banged against the framework. He gasped as the sudden stop nearly wrenched his shoulder out of its socket. His fingers slipped and he fell again. He grabbed the next rung with both hands and held.

The crowd screamed. His feet scrambled for a perch. He twisted his head and discovered that he and Lujinet Nin were hanging back to back. The Imeten was holding on with both hands, too. He was gasping for breath and both sheaths on his back were empty.

Harold jerked his mace off his belt. Lujinet Nin looked

back and Harold swung at him across the void with all the strength left in his aching arms.

Lujinet Nin dropped away from the blow. He stopped himself two rungs below and looked up. His chest was heaving. He leaned his forehead against the framework as if he wanted to take some of the weight off his arms and legs.

Harold looked down. His head slumped onto his chest. The emotions evoked by the fall were still raging through his body. He looked down the open shaft created by the uprights and cringed. Of all the bad dreams he had lived through, that had been the worst.

He jumped off the rung and dropped.

His stomach turned over. The framework flashed by. Lujinet Nin looked up and the first signs of shock and surprise appeared on his face.

Panic hammered at Harold's self-control. He swung with all his might and the mace crashed into the side of Lujinet Nin's head. It slipped out of his hand and he fell toward the next rung with both hands clutching.

His fingers held. Something heavy bounced off his back. He held on and his feet found the lower rung. Below him Lujinet Nin's body banged against the framework as it fell toward the ground. He pressed his face against the back of his hand and closed his eyes.

His lungs sucked in the air. He looked up through the grid and saw the blue sky. Jemil Min appeared at the end of the platform with his two dartblowers crouching by his side.

"The gods have spoken! Obey the gods!"

Horns shrieked. Pans clattered. An Imeten swung through the grid to the bridge and slapped wood before the High Warrior. More Warriors streamed out of the trees after him. A small army crowded onto the upper rungs and let the gods and their leader see they were eager to obey.

Harold stared at them dully. Little by little full awareness